Nantucket in Bloom

A Nantucket Sunset Series

Katie Winters

D1712844

ALL RIGHTS RESERVED. No part of this publication may be reproduced, distributed, or transmitted in any form or by any means, including photocopying, recording, or other electronic or mechanical methods, without the prior written permission of the publisher.

Copyright © 2023 by Katie Winters

This is a work of fiction. Any resemblance of characters to actual persons, living or dead is purely coincidental. Katie Winters holds exclusive rights to this work. Unauthorized duplication is prohibited.

Chapter One

The apartment in Seattle wasn't a palace. With its single room, its view of the trash cans out the back window, and no working stove, Anna Crawford was more than slightly nervous about giving her mother a video tour when she called. As the oldest of the Crawford children, Anna put significant pressure on herself in her career and her personal life— and the crummy apartment, which was the only one she could afford, let alone find in such a difficult market, wasn't exactly how she wanted to present herself.

"But don't worry. I've already called the landlord about the stove," Anna explained after the tour. "And I'm sure I'll be able to find something better by next year." Anna winced at how frightened she sounded.

On her phone screen, Julia was small and smiley, sitting in a sunbeam on Nantucket Island. "Oh, honey. It's your first place by yourself. We all start somewhere."

Anna perched at the edge of her bed as her heart ballooned in her chest.

"I mean it, honey," her mother continued. "Things were

different for me because I met your father so young. But you? You're twenty-three and at the very beginning of your writing career. Be patient with yourself."

Anna's smile matched her mother's, even this far west across the continent. If there was anything the Copperfield Family of Nantucket Island had taught her, it was that life was long and apt to change and alter its course at any moment. It was important to enjoy every season you were in.

"Just don't have a surprise pregnancy like your father and I did," Julia said with a small laugh. "We had to grow up very quickly. If we'd been in a little place like yours, it wouldn't have been pretty."

Anna laughed. "I'm sorry about that."

"It's not completely your fault," Julia teased. "Besides, it all worked out in the end, didn't it? And your story will, too."

After Julia headed out to finish editing a manuscript for her publishing house, which was now vibrant and successful in the wake of Bernard Copperfield's first book in over thirty years, Anna dropped to her knees in front of her suitcase and began to do something she'd always dreamed of doing: she packed for her very first trip away as a travel writer.

Anna piled a sweater, hiking boots, jeans, leggings, workout clothes, and toiletries into her suitcase, thinking about how, as a girl, she'd written stories of faraway lands, imagining what the landscape in Antarctica was like, or what really lurked at the top of Mount Everest. Now, it was her job to go to faraway places, experience them, and write them down for other people as a way for them to experience them, too, if only in story form. It was a dream come true.

There was a knock at the door. Anna hurried up to open it to find Dean wearing that devilishly handsome smile of his. "There she is. The famous travel writer, Anna Crawford." He took a delicate step in, his blue eyes glistening. "I wonder if she'll run off and forget about the people she left behind?"

Anna wrapped her arms loosely around Dean's waist. "Unfortunately for my career, I'm a bit attached to this handsome teacher I know here in Seattle. I can't stay away for long."

"Who is this handsome teacher?" Dean feigned anger. "I'd like to tell him he's not good enough for you."

Anna kissed him, then tugged him deeper into the apartment, giddy with laughter and love. She and Dean had met last summer and found themselves wrapped up in a whirlwind romance. After their second date, they'd hardly spent a day apart, except for when Anna visited her family in Nantucket. Once, Dean had managed to come with her, spending a weekend feasting on Greta's cooking, chatting to Bernard about his philosophies on teaching, walking the beaches, and falling deeper in love with Nantucket (and, Anna knew, with her).

"This is a huge assignment," Anna groaned as she zipped her suitcase. "I don't know if I can do it."

"You're up for it," Dean told her. "I've never met a better writer than you, you know."

Anna grimaced. "You have to say that."

"I don't have to say anything." Dean placed his hand on her shoulder and rubbed it tenderly. "I fell in love with your brain during our very first conversation, and you've been a surprise to me ever since. Besides, didn't your new boss at the travel magazine swoon over your first article?"

"I should have written something worse," Anna suggested. "Now, anything I do will seem lackluster in comparison."

"That's impossible," Dean said kindly.

Dean carried Anna's suitcase to her beat-up car, which she planned to drive to the ferry that would ultimately take her to Orcas Island. With its rocky coastline, its thick emerald pines, and its adorable towns, Orcas Island was a perfect vacation destination for explorers, families, and foodies alike— and Anna had been assigned to write about a brand-new restaurant that was getting buzz in the town center. Her editor had told

3

her to meet up with a friend of his, another travel writer named Everett, who'd lived on Orcas Island since last year and written about it extensively since. Anna planned to meet Everett that evening for dinner and hoped he would give her the ultimate "secret" about how to become a successful travel writer, one who could make traveling, eating, hiking, drinking good wine, and shopping a non-stop lifestyle. To Anna, travel writing seemed the most glamorous life of all.

Dean placed the suitcase in the trunk and kissed Anna with such tenderness that she felt weak in the knees.

"I'll miss you, you know," Dean whispered.

"I'll miss you back," Anna said.

"You're staying at the Harbor Inn?"

"Yes," Anna affirmed. "I'll probably check in by five or so, then head over to meet Everett and his fiancé."

Dean's eyes glistened, and he cupped her hands in his and then kissed her fingers gently. Anna's heart lifted, and she was again struck with the solid realization that one day, she would marry this man. There was no other way.

Anna drove from Seattle to Anacortes, where a ferry awaited to take her to Orcas Island. She parked her car in the belly of the ferry, then locked it and hurried out to the top desk to watch as land receded along the horizon behind her. A shiver raced up her spine.

This was it; she was really doing it. At twenty-three years old, she was in love, chasing her career dreams, and out on an adventure all by herself.

Just before Orcas Island appeared in the distance, Anna's little sister, Rachel, texted from the University of Michigan.

> RACHEL: Hey Anna! Good luck tonight on Orcas Island!
>
> RACHEL: It's so exciting!

Anna smiled into her phone and typed back a thank you. She then studied her little sister's profile picture on the messenger app, which showed a beautiful young woman just a few years younger than Anna. They'd been raised together with their brother, Henry, in a suburb of Chicago called Bartlett. Anna hadn't been back to Bartlett in just about a year, at which time her father, Jackson Crawford, had told his family he'd taken a position in China. Little did Anna and her siblings know that Jackson's announcement of the job change had also served as a divorce announcement. Her parents' divorce had been officially finalized at the end of the previous year.

News of her father's abandonment of her mother had shattered Anna's heart. Since Jackson's departure, she'd hardly spoken to him at all and had told Dean that, in many ways, she felt she no longer had a father.

Once Julia had arrived on Nantucket, however, she'd reconnected with her high school sweetheart, Charlie, with whom she'd fled to New York City at the age of seventeen. Charlie was a professional carpenter, incredibly handsome, with two girls of his own. His wife had passed away a few years ago, which meant that both he and Julia returned to one another, battered and bruised. Together, they worked on healing from the tremendous pain of their past.

It was just about the most romantic thing Anna knew.

Anna drove her car from the ferry and onto Orcas Island with the windows cracked. The breeze through the car was fresh and clean, smelling of pines and salt water. Anna imagined several years down the road when perhaps she and Dean would bring their children here to hike, swim, and eat delicious seafood. She imagined Dean with a toddler on his knee, laughing at Anna with immense joy reflecting from his face.

Anna parked behind the Harbor Inn and hauled her suitcase to the front desk, where a chipper woman in her forties greeted her and checked her into her room. Because Anna still wasn't an "important" travel writer, her editor had booked her a small room with a double bed and a view of the parking lot. Anna took a photograph of it and sent it to Dean, saying, "Maybe in ten years, they'll give me a room by the sea." Dean wrote back with a laughing emoji and said, "At least the sea is only a few minutes' walk away."

Anna, dressed in a black turtleneck and a pair of dark green pants, slid golden earrings into her ears, spritzed herself with perfume, then hurried out the door to meet Everett and his fiancé. Anna walked down Main Street as the sky cooled to a hazy bluish green, and bars and restaurants snapped on their welcoming orange lights. Behind windows, tourists and locals alike sat at thick wooden tables and pinched lemons over slabs of pink salmon, dining to their hearts' content.

Everett had agreed to meet Anna at the very restaurant she'd been asked to review, as he already had a good relationship with the owner and could make a nice introduction. Anna stepped through the thick door and into the warmth of the restaurant, scanning the tops of diners' heads for the sight of Everett, whom she'd only seen photographs of in travel magazines and his website. Previously, Everett had been a sought-after photographer and had even cut his teeth taking photographs of celebrities before he'd switched careers to write full-time.

"Anna?" A confident voice boomed behind her, and Anna turned to find Everett and a beautiful woman in her forties smiling at her. "I thought that was you," Everett continued. "We just got here. We didn't mean to creep up on you."

Anna laughed and stretched out her hand to shake his. "It's so good to meet you in person!"

Everett nodded. "You too. It's so awesome you could make it out." He said it as though he meant it, which was a rare thing in the world of arts, Anna knew. "This is my fiancé, Charlotte."

Charlotte shook Anna's hand next and complimented her

writing. "Your recent article blew me away. I told Everett he better watch his back."

Anna felt herself blush and was unsure of what to say. Luckily, the server approached to seat them, and the three of them were soon at the most beautiful table, which featured a view of the harbor. After they ordered drinks, Everett told her that previously, he'd lived out on Martha's Vineyard with Charlotte but that he hadn't been able to turn down the job on Orcas Island.

"Martha's Vineyard! You're kidding!" Anna felt herself open up. "A lot of my family live on Nantucket."

"No way." Charlotte leaned forward. "I was born and raised on Martha's Vineyard. Were you born and raised on Nantucket?"

"Not quite," Anna explained. "It's a long story."

Everett spread his hands out above the table. "We have all night."

The server arrived with their drinks and a few appetizers, at which time he explained the owner wasn't there that evening — and asked if they wouldn't mind coming back tomorrow for the interview. "He's very sorry. Something came up."

"Of course," Anna assured him. "It'll be good to get a feel for the menu before I speak with him, anyway."

Everett's eyes twinkled. "I see you already have good instincts around being a travel writer."

"I don't know about that." Anna sipped her chardonnay, letting the flavor roll over her tongue. "But goodness, this wine is divine!"

"Isn't it? I can't get enough of this place," Charlotte said. "Every time I come out to visit, I demand we come here."

Anna's smile widened.

"So, tell us," Everett urged. "What is this 'long story' about why you weren't raised on Nantucket?"

"Well, my grandparents raised my mother and her siblings

there," Anna tried, stumbling into the story. "But in the nineties, my grandfather was wrongfully accused of stealing millions of dollars from friends and associates on the island, and..."

"No!" Everett was stick-straight in his chair.

"Your grandfather is Bernard Copperfield?" Charlotte looked aghast.

Anna winced. "So, everyone knows him?"

"Everyone knows him," Charlotte affirmed. "He's mythologized around Martha's Vineyard."

"The nerve of that Marcia Conrad," Everett shot. "I can't believe she's not in jail for what she did."

Anna sighed. "I know. It's horrible, isn't it? But my mom led the charge in proving my grandfather's innocence. She's the one who published his book, as well."

"You come from a pretty impressive family," Everett complimented. "But I have a feeling you didn't use any of their names to get to where you are today."

Anna thought back to her studio apartment back in Seattle, where she couldn't even make ramen noodles on the stove. "I like the idea of being recognized for my own talent rather than my connections to my family."

No way would she mention her father, Jackson Crawford. It was almost a sure thing they'd heard of him, as he'd been the most-viewed nightly news anchor throughout the late winter and had been instrumental in putting cousin Scarlet's boyfriend, Owen, behind bars. But Jackson was someone Anna wanted to wash her hands off completely. It just had to be that way.

"And what do you do, Charlotte?" Anna asked.

Charlotte laughed and squeezed Everett's upper arm. "I'm just a wedding planner."

Everett scoffed. "She's not just a wedding planner. She's planned some of the most elaborate weddings I've ever experienced. She's in such demand that she's booked months in advance. She's just being modest. It's actually how we met. I was on Martha's Vineyard to photograph Ursula..."

"Pennington?" Anna shrieked. "That was such a dramatic-looking wedding! I was fascinated with it when it happened." Anna had been in college at the time and had scoured magazine pages, obsessing over the celebrity wedding with her girlfriends. It had been a different time.

"Ursula had plenty of money to play around with," Charlotte breathed. "But ultimately, she and her fiancé were married in a tiny church, not far from the swankier location they'd initially picked."

"And Charlotte and I were the only ones in the audience," Everett said, eyeing Charlotte lovingly.

"That's beautiful," Anna said, dropping her gaze.

"And you, Anna? Are you seeing anyone?" Charlotte asked brightly.

Anna felt herself gushing. "I started seeing a middle school teacher last summer. He's from Ohio originally but moved out to Seattle for college. He swept me off my feet."

Charlotte's eyes were alight. "If you ever need a wedding planner, just say the word."

"Thank you. I don't know how we could ever afford you, but thank you." Anna's heart swelled.

The food came soon afterward, taking their minds off of the far-away islands of Nantucket and Martha's Vineyard. Anna ate her weight in salmon, mussels, roasted potatoes, savory salads, and a tantalizing creme brûlée, and then admitted she was stuffed full.

"I'll be back tomorrow," Anna said after they'd paid the bill. "I can try the rest of the menu, then."

"How long are you staying?" Everett asked as they stood to leave.

"I'll be here for about a week," Anna explained. "My editor

wants me to get a good feel for the island and scout for more stories."

"Let me know if you need any help," Everett said. "I don't like the idea that journalists are so secretive about their stories and tips. We need to help each other, you know?"

"That's wonderful," Anna replied. "I have a hunch you're one of the only journalists who feels that way."

"He is," Charlotte said, wrinkling her nose.

On the street, Charlotte hugged Anna goodbye, and Everett shook her hand, congratulating her again on her previous article and her newfound career. Anna then floated back to her hotel, sensing that this was one of the best nights of her entire life. She was on top of the world.

Chapter Two

Anna entered the Harbor Inn reception area, shivering from the sharp chill of the April evening. The woman behind the desk greeted her by name and smiled. "Hello, Anna. I hope you had a wonderful dinner?"

Anna paused and smiled back, grateful for the friendly welcome. "It was absolutely delicious. This place is pretty magical, isn't it?"

"It is. I hope the rest of your stay is just as magical, if not more."

"Thank you," Anna said. "Goodnight."

Anna hurried up to her bedroom with its view of the parking lot, laughing to herself about how ridiculously wonderful it all was. When she reached the door, she slid her key into the lock, already planning a hot bath, podcast, and then bedtime soon after.

Anna pressed the door open, stepped into the room, and immediately shrieked. There, seated on the edge of her bed, was the shadowy outline of a man. She whipped her hand to the left to turn on the light to reveal none other than Dean, her handsome boyfriend, who sat on her bed surrounded by what looked to be one hundred roses. Anna's knees were weak.

"Dean?"

Dean's eyes shimmered with longing. He stood from her bed, adjusting his suit jacket as he approached her gently. "I didn't mean to frighten you."

Anna's heart swelled with joy. Slowly, she closed the door behind her and took a step toward him, understanding that this moment wasn't one she wanted to forget. Not ever. She had to find a way to remember every single second.

Dean leafed into his suit pocket and removed a very small velvet box. Anna's throat was tight, so much so that she wasn't sure she could speak. "Dean..." she finally managed to say again, her voice raspy.

Dean dropped to one knee in front of her and took her left hand with his. "Anna, I love you."

Anna felt on the verge of falling to her knees before him, if only because she wasn't sure her legs would support her a moment longer. "I love you, too."

"And I love the life we've built together so far," Dean continued.

"Me too." Anna's hand shivered in his.

"The moment I met you, I knew my life was different," Dean breathed. "Beforehand, I'd never experienced real, true love— the kind that isn't self-serving and takes no record of wrongs. But with you, even early on, I felt that our love was the truest thing of all. And I would love to keep building that love and our life together. If you'll have me."

Anna's shoulders were slack. All of her life, she'd envisioned a gorgeous engagement like this— yet she'd never thought it would come so soon. She was twenty-three and at the very beginning of her career. Her stove didn't even work, for crying out loud.

But she knew in her heart that none of that mattered. Not

as long as she and Dean had one another.

"Ask me!" Anna cried suddenly, laughing as Dean's smile widened.

"You're impatient," Dean returned. "I've always loved that about you, too." He then swallowed and asked, "Anna Crawford. Will you make me the happiest man in the world and marry me?"

Anna did drop to her knees after that. She threw her arms around him, whispered, "Yes! Of course I will," and kissed him with her eyes closed. Around them, the rest of the world carried on with their lives as Anna and Dean solidified the only thing they truly needed: one another.

Afterward, Anna and Dean collapsed on the bed of the hotel and held one another, gazing at the glitz of Anna's engagement ring and into one another's eyes. Outside, a steady rain had begun to fall, and it soon mounted into a downpour, the raindrops pelting against the window. Anna cuddled closer to Dean and finally heard herself asking him about the logistics of the proposal.

"I asked the hotel receptionist over a week ago if I could do this," he explained. "She was so excited."

"She acted like she was up to something downstairs," Anna said.

"She has already received an epic tip for her help," Dean added with a laugh. "She helped me bring all the roses to the room, as well."

"I can't believe it." Anna closed her eyes for a moment as, suddenly, Dean stood from the bed and hustled for the mini-fridge. There, he took out a bottle of champagne and wagged his eyebrows.

"Let's make a toast to our future," Dean said.

Anna bounced up and grabbed two plastic cups from the bathroom, the ones normally reserved for brushing your teeth. The plastic cups and the champagne seemed to perfectly reflect the state of their current relationship. They were young, mostly broke, and willing to make anything work.

Dean uncorked the champagne, and bubbles floated down the neck before he poured.

"Dean?" Anna surprised herself with her own voice. "You're the love of my life."

Dean's eyes widened, and he hurried forward to kiss her on the lips. "You're the love of my life." He then filled the plastic glasses, which they clinked together and drank from. Anna's mind swirled with ecstasy.

Long after midnight, after they'd drunk the rest of the bottle of champagne and talked about their love till they were blue in the face, Anna sighed and said, "Do you have to go back to school tomorrow?"

Dean shook his head mischievously. "I have the rest of the week off."

Anna's jaw dropped. "You're kidding!"

"Come on, Anna. This is one of the biggest milestones in our lives. I figured we could eat our weight in the local food, go hiking, and make friends with the locals. Maybe we can even pretend we live here."

Anna's heart opened with happiness. "Dean! Thank you." She threw her arms around him, as she knew it wasn't an easy thing to get time off from the school he worked at.

"Who knows where we'll end up, Anna," Dean said wistfully. "Maybe we'll want to raise our children somewhere like this. Or maybe, just maybe, we'll end up back on Nantucket with your family."

Anna sighed and placed her ear against his chest to hear its sturdy beat. He wrapped his arms around her, comfort against the chaos of the rest of the world. They were twenty-three and twenty-five with so much of their lives in front of them. It was remarkable to know that the rest of their lives had begun right there, in a very tiny room on Orcas Island.

Chapter Three

Eloise Richards Clemmens lived alone on the Clemmens Farm on the outskirts of Muncie, Indiana. She'd lived there alone for three years since the death of her husband, Liam, who'd grown up on the farm and, after they'd met in the seventies, brought her there to live with him. Eloise had prayed for a beautiful future together, that they would have children, raise them on the farm, and live an honest yet happy life. Unfortunately, children had never come, and happiness had come in fits and starts.

It was a beautiful afternoon in April, in the upper sixties, and Eloise stood in a pair of overalls and gazed across the flat fields that surrounded the farmhouse and the barn. Sunlight sparkled against the dead weeds, which cut out from the soft spring earth. Since Liam's death, she hadn't had the energy to keep the farm going, and she'd hired other farmers to handle the land themselves, taking most of the profit along with them. But Eloise made more than enough to get by.

Then again, Eloise was only sixty-five years old. It was

possible she'd be at the Clemmens Farm all alone for the next twenty years. The thought chilled her to the bone.

Eloise walked back into the farmhouse to make herself a cup of tea and read the newspaper. In it, journalists wrote at-length about the rainy season, the soybean crops, and the local basketball and baseball teams. Eloise had been an Indiana resident since the seventies, but a part of her had always felt separate from all of it, as though she was reading a book but didn't quite understand the language it was written in.

"You're a Hoosier, through and through!" Liam had told her many times over the years, especially on their happier days together. "I can't remember Indiana before you were in it."

But it wasn't true. Eloise still had dreams about her youth, when she'd been a girl on Nantucket Island— a gorgeous, sun-dappled place lined with white, sandy beaches and filled with rolling green hills and beautiful daffodils. She hadn't been there since she was sixteen years old, but when she used the computer in the study, she googled images of the place and realized, with a lurch in her stomach, that her memories of Nantucket weren't that far off. It really was heaven on earth.

The fact that she'd had to leave the island continued to shatter her heart, no matter how often she told herself it didn't matter. "It is what it is," is what she'd previously said about it. Unfortunately, even so many years after the fact, her departure was still the single-most horrific event of her life.

As the sun began to drop in the late-afternoon sky and fill the house with orange light, Eloise grabbed her spring jacket and walked out to Liam's truck, which she'd enjoyed using since his death. High up in the driver's seat, she was able to pretend she had a level of power that she really didn't. She'd sold her car two years ago for a measly three thousand dollars to some high school kid who'd been very pleased with his newfound freedom. Her friends had thought she was nuts. "Who wants to drive such a big truck?" they'd asked.

Harlequin Presents®

Retail Value: $5.99-$7.25 USD

AVAILABLE IN REGULAR AND LARGER PRINT

The Maid's Pregnancy Bombshell *by Lynne Graham*

The Greek only needed a bride! Now he has a baby on the way in this accidental-pregnancy romance by *USA TODAY* bestselling author Lynne Graham..

Regular Print: 8CPW ◆ Larger Print: 8CQE

BONUS BUCKS CATALOG

Eloise drove the truck into Muncie, where she shopped at Kroger, filling her cart with enough food for the rest of the week — yogurt, cereal, fruits, vegetables, and even a kind of pasta made with chickpeas, which interested her. Since Liam's death, Eloise had hardly eaten any of the things she'd previously cooked for him, like steak and pork chops. It was strange, she thought now, the little things that changed when your partner in life left you behind. She'd lost a bit of weight, yes— but she'd lost some strength, too.

Eloise's friend, Brenda, texted just before she headed out of town.

> BRENDA: Eloise! It's been such a long time since we last spoke. Would you like to come over for coffee and catch up?

Eloise wrote back immediately, pleased to have been thought of. She hated to admit how lonely she was and very rarely reached out to the friends she and Liam once had together.

> ELOISE: I'm in town. I could come by now.

Brenda sent back an "okay," and Eloise started the engine in the truck and headed over to Brenda's house off of Main Street. Traffic had escalated, and Eloise cursed herself for shopping so late. Muncie wasn't an average town in Indiana. It was home to Ball State University, and it seemed to triple in size at certain hours of the day as professors and students swarmed from the campus.

Brenda was out on the front porch when Eloise drove up in the truck. She raised a hand and smiled gently as Eloise stepped out of the truck and walked toward her. "Look at those overalls," Brenda beamed.

"I'm a farm girl," Eloise joked as she hugged Brenda close, surprised at how easy it seemed to hug her after so many weeks without human touch.

In the house, Brenda prepared a pot of coffee and sliced pieces of lemon cake, upon which she'd drizzled a light frosting.

"Mike likes there to be something sweet when he comes home," Brenda explained.

"I remember those days," Eloise offered, thinking of when Liam had come in from a hard day in the fields. "Liam used to bark and rage with hunger. Once he was fed, he fell asleep like a lost puppy on the couch."

Brenda frowned. "You must miss him so much."

Eloise wasn't sure what to say to that, so she lifted her mug of coffee and sipped. To get the subject off of her and her lonely life, she asked Brenda questions about her grandchildren, and Brenda brightened up immediately. A part of Eloise burned dully with jealousy, but only a part. She'd always imagined herself to have children and grandchildren, but she'd never imagined she'd end up so alone. Those were the cards she'd been dealt.

"You know, Eloise, the girls and I have been talking about you," Brenda said, interrupting Eloise's reverie. "And we think you should sell that farm out there and buy a place in town. We play cards every Wednesday, and you could join us at church on Sundays."

Eloise's stomach tightened at the thought. On the one hand, she'd considered it herself— abandoning that farm on the outskirts and becoming a new and improved version of Eloise here in town. On the other hand, the idea of abandoning Liam's farm after his death made her feel very sad. Liam had wanted to keep the farm in his family so badly that he'd asked her to move back to Indiana with him. When the children hadn't come, Liam's eyes had grown increasingly hollow, so much so that sometimes, when Liam seemed to be looking at Eloise, he wasn't looking at anything at all.

"I'll think about it," Eloise told her.

"You should," Brenda said. "Liam's been gone three years. And you said it yourself..." She trailed off.

Eloise tilted her head. "What did I say myself?"

Brenda wrinkled her nose and took a bite of cake. "I shouldn't have said it."

"Come on, Brenda. You can say anything to me."

Brenda sighed and tapped a napkin across her lips. "After Liam died, you were, of course, very sad."

Eloise furrowed her brow. There was so little she remembered from the time directly after Liam's death.

Brenda went on. "You spoke very little, of course. I don't know what the girls and I expected you to say, not so soon after losing your husband. But you did mention something that surprised us. You said that Liam wasn't the love of your life. That you'd already been in love, real love, but that you'd had to turn your back on it."

Eloise raised her eyebrows. That was something she thought she'd never told anyone. She supposed that in her grief after Liam's death, she'd allowed a few thoughts to the surface, ones she shouldn't have.

"I don't suppose it matters who the love of my life was," Eloise answered. "I was married to Liam for decades. That has to count for something."

Brenda dropped her gaze, clearly embarrassed. "Of course. Liam was your life. We understand that." She paused again, then went on as though pushing herself before she chickened out. "You're young, Eloise. There's so much life for you left. Maybe you could even meet someone here in town. The girls and I know plenty of divorcées."

"That's very kind of you," Eloise said, bristling at the idea of going on a date as a sixty-five-year-old woman. *What on earth would she wear? Her overalls? One of Liam's big sweaters?* She had nothing, clothing-wise, that made her feel like a youthful and vibrant woman. She'd made her peace with being a widow. That was the hand she'd been dealt.

Eloise finished her cake and eventually found her way back to Liam's truck. From the driver's seat, she waved to Brenda, then dropped her foot on the pedal and pulled herself out of there. The traffic had cleared slightly, and she found herself turning out onto the country road all alone, with the haze of the spring evening folding into pastels around her. She cracked the window of the truck and leaned her head back so that the wind cut through her gray curls.

And then, she smelled it.

It was the smell of smoke, of ash. Eloise dropped her foot on the brake and slowed, inhaling deeper through her nose. At the very edge of each breath, the smell of smoke intensified to the smell of burning — of melted steel, of burning wood.

Next came the sirens. In her rear-view, two fire trucks skidded into the country road and burst to the left of her, followed by two cop cars. Eloise wanted to close her eyes and tell herself it couldn't be the Clemmens Farm; there was no way.

But a deeper, secret part of herself knew. She just knew.

Eloise drove slowly down the country road until she could see the Clemmens Farm around the curve of the road. Sure enough, there it was: over one hundred years of Clemmens family history beneath a violent roar of a flame. Eloise stopped the engine about a half-mile from the farm and watched as the firemen did their best to pound water onto the farmhouse, but already, the second story had splintered away and left only a charred skeleton of the first floor.

It was remarkable to watch your entire life go up in flames, Eloise thought. Even now, she thought of everything in those walls— everything she'd just recently lost. All of Liam's shirts

20

were burnt to a crisp. The few items she'd brought with her from Nantucket were gone. The computer, books, an antique table, and even the painting on the wall that she'd made back in 1988 when she'd taken a painting class at Ball State University. It was all gone in the blink of an eye.

Slowly, Eloise reached for her cell and dialed Brenda's number, as she wasn't sure who else to call.

"Eloise? Did you forget something?" Brenda asked, her voice chipper.

Eloise sighed, then heard herself begin to laugh. "Brenda? I'm beginning to think that place in town isn't such a bad idea."

At that moment, one of the windows in the downstairs of the farmhouse burst, shattering glass across the lawn.

"That's so good to hear!" Brenda said. "I knew you'd come around."

Eloise sniffed as tears came to her eyes. She hadn't realized how much she'd relied on this farm. It had been lonely, but it had been all hers.

"I'll talk to you soon, Brenda. Maybe we can look at houses together?"

"I'd like that very much," Brenda returned. "I'll call you tomorrow."

Chapter Four

Anna and Dean's week on Orcas Island was nothing but blissful. Together, they feasted at the inn's breakfast buffet, roamed the fields, forests, and beaches, dined at the restaurant Anna needed to write about, along with several others, spoke to locals, and drank at classic Orcas Island bars. Everywhere they went, Dean, practiced saying, "This is my fiancée, Anna," and Anna practiced saying, "This is my fiancé, Dean," and each time, they giggled about it, as though they shared a secret that nobody on the planet could ever understand.

On the day before they planned to return to Seattle, Anna and Dean met Everett and Charlotte for breakfast. Charlotte was headed back to Martha's Vineyard that afternoon to reunite with her daughter, who was in her final few months of high school.

"It'll be hard to say goodbye to Martha's Vineyard," Charlotte said as she drew her fingers through her hair, flashing her own engagement ring. "But Orcas Island is ripe for discovery."

"And you'll be back to visit your siblings all the time," Everett assured her.

Charlotte smiled at Anna and again raised Anna's hand from the table to assess her engagement ring. Although it was much smaller than Charlotte's, Anna's heart ballooned with love for it. This was the size Dean could afford right now, and it was the size Anna would wear for the rest of her days. *What did she need a big rock for?* She had all the love in the world.

"Have you called your family on Nantucket to tell them the big news yet?" Charlotte asked.

Anna shook her head. "No. We've selfishly kept the news to ourselves."

"We know, once we tell them, we'll have to be on the phone for hours and hours to explain how it happened and what our plans are," Dean explained.

"And all we've really wanted to do since it happened was spend time with each other," Anna said.

Charlotte and Everett exchanged joyful glances, as though they were enlivened by the happiness between Anna and Dean.

"Remember," Charlotte said. "I'm a wedding planner. You'd better give me a call when you're ready to start planning." She slid her business card across the table, and Anna pocketed it, smiling to herself.

After breakfast, Dean and Anna went back to the inn to change clothes and head out on a hike. Anna had finished her article for her travel magazine last night, and as she changed, her phone pinged with an email from her editor, who said the article was "one of the best things he'd ever read." Anna swooned and fell onto the bed as Dean bounced onto the mattress beside her.

"What? You look like you might float away." Dean kissed her gently on the cheek.

Anna showed Dean the email, and Dean cried out with

excitement and covered her with more kisses. "I told you they'd love it."

"You don't have to be right all the time." Anna stuck out her tongue.

"I don't have to be," Dean teased. "But I mostly am, especially when it comes to your success."

With their hiking boots on, Anna and Dean hurried down the old-fashioned circular staircase of the Harbor Inn and burst into the bright light that seeped from behind the Pacific Northwest's gruesome clouds.

"Do you think it's going to rain?" Anna asked.

Dean shrugged. "I don't know! Should we brave it?"

Anna thought for a moment. "We'll both be strapped to our indoor jobs for the next month. We should take advantage of our time off."

"That's what I like to hear. Besides, we've both lived in Seattle for a while now. We can't let a little rain scare us," Dean said.

Anna and Dean made their way from town back toward the trails They walked hand-in-hand, often quiet, their boots shuffling against the wet grass and stepping through the mud as carefully as they could.

Soon, the path lifted in elevation, up and up so that their thighs screamed. Dean laughed up ahead of Anna and said, "I should do that Stairmaster thing at the gym more often."

"That thing is the worst!" Anna called back.

"Maybe we really should move out here," Dean suggested. "We could hike this trail every day and get huge, muscular thighs."

"I still want to fit into my skinny jeans, thanks," Anna joked.

Dean stopped, turned, and smiled at her. "Nobody looks better in skinny jeans than you do."

Anna's cheeks burned with a mix of embarrassment and

pleasure. "Dean!" She hurried up and swatted him. "Don't tease me."

Dean kissed her with his eyes closed, then grabbed her hand and began to run up the mountain so that Anna squealed as she struggled to catch up. As they went, rain began to fall from the heavens above, dripping from the leaves overhead and flattening across their foreheads and cheeks. Already, Anna's black hair hung in wet streaks down her back, and Dean's was wadded across his forehead.

When they reached the top of an embankment, they huddled under thick tree branches for a moment's rest from the rain. There, they kissed as the rain came down faster and faster. Anna finally laughed and said, "I don't know. Maybe we should turn back?"

Dean grimaced. "We were too confident, I guess." He leafed through his pocket to find his phone. "Maybe I can download a weather app and see when the rain is supposed to end."

"Thank you," Anna said. A chill crept across her neck, and she zipped her jacket up to her chin.

As the app downloaded, Dean turned, wrapped one hand around the trunk of a tree, and peered down at the monstrous cliff directly beside them. The cliff was rocky and jagged, and it slanted down toward a thick blanket of emerald green treetops. Anna shivered.

"It's gorgeous up here," Dean said. He then glanced at his phone again and removed his hand from the tree trunk. "Ah. Looks like the rain will cut out in forty-five minutes."

"Oh no!" Anna laughed and dropped her head.

"Too long to be stuck in the woods with me?"

Anna rolled her eyes and stepped into him, allowing him to hold her. For a little while, he sang a song into her ear, one they always played on the radio as they drove through late-night Seattle on their way from one thing to another. The song reminded her of the coziness of their union, how they needed no one but one another.

Dean's phone pinged, and he dropped his arms to check it. "The rain app added another ten minutes to the rain," he said with a laugh.

Anna shrugged. "Maybe we'll just get married up here."

"We can have the ceremony right here on this cliff," Dean said. "And I can build us a log cabin over there!" He pointed along the edge of the trail, where the moist ground lifted to support a thick line of trees. "We can raise our children in this very forest. They won't need schools or communities or anything but the great outdoors."

"Great," Anna said with a laugh. "Are you suggesting our children will be illiterate?"

Dean shrugged. "I don't know how to read. I'm doing all right for myself."

Anna's jaw dropped. "What—"

At this, Dean bowed over with laughter. "The look on your face! I can't believe you believed me for a second!"

Anna blushed and leaned against the thick tree. "Yeah, yeah. I need to get rid of that gullible side of myself, otherwise, I'm going to get eaten alive in the travel writing world."

Dean placed his hand on her cheek. "You're going to be incredible, babe."

A few minutes later, the rain seemed to double. It pounded against the leaves, dug crevices in the soil beneath them, and shattered across the rocks that stuck out from the cliff beneath.

Dean had grown impatient. He paced the edge of the cliffs, eyeing the treetops below them and the thick clouds above.

"Dean? Will you step back a little bit?" Anna's voice was meek.

Dean glanced her way and smiled. "I'm fine, Anna. These hiking boots are sturdy." He took several steps to the other side of the tree and then pointed out toward the water, where a lighthouse stood, powerful against the ominous winds and rain. "If you could have told little old me back in Ohio that I'd eventually end up here, I would have called you a liar."

Anna laughed. "Me too, back when I was in Illinois."

Dean took a small step forward, his eyes gleaming with the soft light that beamed out from the rainclouds. Anna was captivated by him. She grabbed her cell from her pocket and quickly took several photographs, which made Dean laugh.

"You know I hate getting my picture taken," Dean said.

Anna blushed. "That means I have to be sneaky."

It happened all at once, after that— during this impossible moment when Anna thought for sure that their love was strong enough to last forever. The ground beneath Dean's feet began to crumble, as though it was brownie batter. It tumbled off the edge of the cliff, knocking Dean off balance.

"DEAN!" Anna cried as she lurched toward him.

Dean's eyes looked panicked. His arms laced through the air in front of him as he fell, disappearing quickly through the air and going down with the rain.

Anna gasped and fell to her knees. Everything in her told her this couldn't be happening, that this was a nightmare and not real. But the ground beneath her knees was soft and wet, and the rain continued to plant itself on her head, and she was suddenly sickly aware that something horrible had just happened.

"Dean!" Anna hurried to the edge of the cliff and peered down, searching for some sign of him. There was no way she could get down there to find him herself— the cliff was way too slippery to climb down.

Still, a part of her wanted to do it. A part of her almost demanded her to do it.

Instead, Anna dialed the local emergency services. A panicked voice that she soon recognized as her own explained which trail she was on and what had happened. A man on the line told her to stay where she was and that a helicopter would be sent shortly. Anna begged the man to stay on the line with her, and the man agreed.

"He was right here," Anna said into the phone.

"I know. And we're sending someone to come find him," the man assured her.

"You don't understand. We're getting married." Anna screamed with fear.

"Can you focus on your breathing, ma'am?" the man asked her. "I know it's hard. Maybe we can breathe together."

But Anna couldn't breathe. She could do nothing but stare far off toward the horizon, where the same lighthouse Dean had commented on moments ago began to roll its lights across the rainy gray day. Her heart was in her throat. Somewhere deep in her body, she knew that nothing in her life would ever be the same again— that everything had been forever changed.

These were the first moments of the rest of her life. What a fool she'd been to think she could be happy.

Chapter Five

Two days after the fire, Eloise moved into a temporary apartment five streets away from Brenda's house. The apartment was fully furnished, with a microwave that made food limp and lukewarm, a double bed that was stiff as a board, and a flatscreen television that brought live news and sitcoms to the very small and impersonal living room every single night.

Eloise was not sure how to feel in the wake of the fire. She'd checked into a hotel on the night it had happened and slept in her overalls on top of the sheets, dreaming of Liam, of his mother who had baked bread in that kitchen that was now no more, and about Liam's grandmother, who'd given birth in the living room on a hot summer's day so many years ago. *What had happened to all those stories?* Eloise was the only person in the world who carried them— and she was hardly a Clemmens herself.

Brenda and her friends brought Eloise baked goods and lasagnas, their eyes moist and worried as they asked her how Eloise was. Eloise thought they maybe suspected her as the arsonist, as though there was money to be had for insurance purposes, which there wasn't. Eloise didn't go out of her way to tell them it had been an electrical fire, with no fault. She sort-of liked how suspicious they were of her. They looked at her as though she could combust any minute.

Brenda, of course, didn't suspect her in the slightest— but she was worried that Eloise hadn't cried yet. The afternoon after Eloise moved in five streets away, Brenda urged her to go to therapy about the fire. To this, Eloise said, "I wasn't there. I didn't lose anyone. This is hardly a tragedy." Brenda hadn't known what to say, so she went into the kitchen and prepared Eloise another pot of soup. Eloise wasn't sure how she was going to get through all the food these dear women had prepared for her. It was as though they had nowhere to put the tremendous amount of love they were able to give the world.

Two days after Eloise moved into the apartment, she sat with a very cold piece of lasagna and watched the nightly news. Recently, Quentin Copperfield had been replaced with a man named Jackson Crawford, who'd then been replaced with a woman Eloise rather liked. It was a rare thing for a woman to read the nightly news, and Eloise relished it— seeing it as proof that women were striving further in their careers every year. She had been born during a time when women's rights were hardly a whisper on people's lips.

Eloise thought the switch from Quentin to Jackson was a funny one, given what she knew about the Copperfield family. Jackson and Quentin had once been brothers-in-law, their connection only legal, with no family ties or love. Now, they were nothing to one another. She knew that— the legal aspects. She didn't know the why or how.

She could glean only so much about the Copperfields from a distance. To her, they were more like fictional characters in a book she'd read as a child. One she'd read obsessively until they'd come to life in her mind.

But on this evening, two days after she'd moved into the nondescript apartment in downtown Muncie, Indiana, the woman who read the news sat at her news desk and reported something terrible.

"Good evening. Tonight, we must honor the life of a young man who was taken too soon— a young man with a connection to us here at the station. This young man's name was Dean Carpenter, and he'd recently asked Anna Crawford, the daughter of one of our anchors here at the station, to marry him. Our hearts go out to Anna, to Dean's family, and to Jackson during this difficult time."

Eloise reached for the remote control and turned off the television. There she sat, in the shadows of this living room that was really not hers, and felt tears finally spring to her eyes. *Was this really the first time she was going to cry in the wake of the fire?* It seemed so. Tears rained down her cheeks and dotted her overalls.

How had this happened? How had a young man like Dean Carpenter died so young before his real life had begun? It seemed so horrific, more proof that the world operated with its own rules and remained unbothered regarding the wants and needs of its people.

Poor Anna Crawford. Eloise knew very little of Anna— only that she was Julia's daughter, that she lived in Seattle, and that she had jet-black hair and very sharp, intelligent eyes. The fact that she'd met the love of her life, only to have him taken away so soon like that, chilled Eloise to the bone. It reminded her of the horrors of her own past.

Brenda had lent Eloise her husband's old computer, and Eloise walked to it now, turned it on, and googled the young man's name. DEAN CARPENTER. The first results told Eloise what had happened that fateful day, the same day Eloise's farm had been aflame. Dean and Anna had gone for a hike on Orcas Island, and Dean had fallen from the cliff's edge.

A medical team had come to collect both Dean and Anna, but Dean's injuries had been severe, and he'd died a little over a day after the accident. Anna had been holding his hand at the time.

None of the articles had any quotes from Anna, which Eloise was glad about. She hoped most journalists had the goodwill to keep away from Anna, to allow her to grieve her love in peace.

Just before Eloise planned to stop reading about Dean and Anna, to perhaps turn on the television to watch one of the sitcoms, she read:

Dean Carpenter's funeral will be held in Dayton, Ohio, on April 12, 2023, with a viewing at two p.m. and a service immediately following at four.

Dayton, Ohio. Eloise's eyes widened. Dayton was not far from where she lived, not in the slightest. Suddenly, a seed of an idea planted itself in her brain, one that she tried to drive out as soon as it appeared.

All these years, Eloise had been more-or-less trapped in the Midwest. All these years, she'd been at the mercy of her memories of those long-lost days in Nantucket. Now, Anna Crawford would be only a few hours away.

Eloise turned off the computer and shook her head. *No,* she thought. She was out of her mind. Anna Crawford didn't know anything about who she was or what she wanted. To Anna, Eloise was just an old lady in a pair of farming overalls, nothing more.

But then again, when else would Eloise get the opportunity to see one of the Copperfields in person? For years, she'd studied them from a distance— her heart shattering at Bernard's prison sentence, championing Alana's modeling career, or weeping at the beauty of the books Julia's publishing house published. She'd never been brave enough to reach out, not even when their world had fallen apart.

Okay. If she did drive to Ohio, what then? Would she just walk up to Anna Crawford and explain everything? No. She wouldn't. The girl was going through the most heinous days of her life. It was an era of constant re-calibration, during which the plans she'd set for herself no longer had anything to do with what would happen in her future. She'd planned to be married, to have a family with Dean Carpenter. Eloise understood that all too well.

When Eloise went to bed that night, she'd more-or-less convinced herself not to drive to Ohio. It was foolish, reckless. No good could possibly come from it.

But then, two days later, she found herself behind the wheel of Liam's truck, headed east toward Dayton. How did this happen? How did she let herself go to Walmart, purchase a black dress and a pair of black flats, smear makeup on her cheeks (something she hadn't done in years!), and disembark? She hadn't told anyone where she was off to. It wasn't a reasonable thing to explain. She could half-imagine Brenda's expression. *"Say what, now? What are you going to do?"*

That wasn't Brenda's fault. Perhaps Eloise should have been more open about her past. In truth, she hadn't even told Liam about what had happened in Nantucket, nor why she'd had to leave. Liam, being Liam, hadn't asked.

The drive to Dayton took about two and a half hours. Eloise turned into the funeral home parking lot, then parked, peered toward the front door of the establishment, and froze with fear. Other mourners had begun to arrive, all dressed in black, their hair gleaming beneath an April sun. Eloise placed her hands over her face as her heart thudded. This wasn't her loss to mourn. She shouldn't have driven here. *What had she been thinking?*

Before she could convince herself to go in to find Anna, Eloise reversed out of the parking lot and sped back onto the main road of Dayton. Her eyes were filled with tears, and it was difficult to see. Three roads down, a diner advertised free re-fills on coffee and grilled cheese sandwiches. Eloise hurriedly pulled into the parking lot, parked, and walked into the diner, where people ate greasy eggs and bacon and read the paper, even this far into the afternoon. It felt like a non-judgmental place. Maybe, had she sat with one of these strangers and explained everything that had happened to her and why she was in Dayton in the first place, they would say, "I understand. Any sane person would understand why you did this."

Eloise mopped herself up in the bathroom and sat in a booth, where she ordered a cup of coffee and a grilled cheese. The black dress she'd gotten from Walmart now seemed so plasticky and bad, and it clung to her body in all the wrong places. All she wanted was to be back in her overalls. All she wanted was to be back home.

Just as Eloise's coffee and grilled cheeses came, the front door of the diner burst open. There, standing in the doorway with red-rimmed eyes and a panicked expression, stood Anna Crawford. Eloise stared at her with her coffee poised near her lips. *Was this real? Was this really happening?* Anna stumbled into the diner and took the booth directly in front of Eloise's but sat facing away from her. She then blew her nose and muffled a sigh into the Kleenex.

The waitress arrived to take Anna's order, which was a coffee and a grilled cheese, just like Eloise's. All the while, Eloise stared into the jet-black hair on the back of Anna's head and considered whether she should run out of the diner, back to her truck, and flee Ohio forever.

Then again, why wasn't Anna at the funeral? Why was she at this rinky-dink diner down the road?

Was this some kind of sign?

Anna's coffee came, but Anna had begun to cry harder, and there didn't seem to be enough napkins on the table or Kleenex in her purse. Eloise took a deep breath, leaned forward, and said, "Excuse me? Miss?"

Anna froze, then turned to glare at Eloise. Obviously, she was embarrassed to have been called out for crying.

Eloise passed her clean handkerchief across the table and nodded toward it. "Have this."

Anna waved her hand. "That's okay."

"Please. I insist."

Anna grimaced, then took the handkerchief and blew her nose. A warmth flooded Eloise. This was the first contact she'd had with a Copperfield, and she'd actually been able to help out.

But soon after, Anna's shoulders began to shake wildly, and it was clear the girl was about to hyperventilate. Eloise leaped to her feet and hurried to her table, where she sat and placed her hand on Anna's shoulder.

"Honey, you need to breathe," Eloise told her.

Anna placed her hand over her chest, and her eyes were elsewhere, unfocused. "I. Can't," she finally managed to say.

"Let's do it together," Eloise coaxed. "Inhale. Exhale." She said it slowly, helping Anna bring oxygen into her lungs, watching as her stomach rose to give space to the lungs.

For nearly ten minutes, Eloise said this, over and over again — inhale, exhale, until finally, Anna was able to breathe again. Throughout, nobody else in the diner said a single thing, as though they worried that they would distract Eloise from her mission. To everyone, Eloise seemed like a stranger who'd stepped in to help. In a way, she was.

The grilled cheese arrived, and Eloise urged Anna to eat. Anna shook her head and sipped her coffee. "I really can't. I'm sorry."

Eloise sighed, remembering that when Liam had died, she'd refused food, too. It had seemed superfluous. *Why should she eat when Liam no longer needed food?*

35

"Honey, you can tell me about what happened," Eloise said softly. "If you think talking will help."

Anna pursed her lips, then sipped her coffee. "I don't know. I don't know how to talk to anyone."

Eloise nodded as Anna's face crumpled up.

"I should be somewhere else right now," Anna continued. "I really need to be somewhere else. But I just can't be there. It's too hard. I can't be there, seeing everyone's eyes on me, pitying me. I can't bear to speak to his parents. Gosh, I hardly even knew his parents! And now, they're just strangers with these empty eyes. When I got here last night, they picked me up from the airport, and I had a panic attack on the way to their house. I didn't know what to do. But the worst of it was, that was my third panic attack yesterday." Anna sipped her coffee again, seeming to come back into herself. "I can't get back on a plane. There's no way. I'm terrified of everything now. Me! I used to be open to every kind of adventure, and now, as soon as the plane takes off down the runway, I have a panic attack. It's incredible."

Eloise rubbed her shoulder timidly. "You seem to have a rational reason to be scared of flying."

Anna puffed her cheeks. "The thing is, I need to get home. I need to get to Nantucket. And it's so, so far." She sounded defeated. "I could take a bus, but..."

"A bus? All the way from here to Nantucket?" Eloise's eyes widened. "You don't want anything to do with that. That would give anyone a panic attack."

"I know. I know." Anna palmed the back of her neck.

Eloise felt another idea coming through her like a storm across a flat Indiana field. She couldn't possibly suggest this. And yet, here it was— a crazy, horrible idea.

"I'm heading out east," Eloise began.

Anna tilted her head. "Oh?"

"Yes. And I always like company on a drive," Eloise

explained quickly, the words coming to her at will. "If you want, you can come with me."

Anna waved both hands in front of her. "No, no. I couldn't do that. I don't want to be a burden."

"You wouldn't be a burden," Eloise explained. She then searched through her purse to remove her driver's license and several other IDs, along with a photograph she kept of herself and Liam during happier days. "Maybe it's better if I explain who I am so that we're not strangers anymore." Eloise managed a small smile, which Anna tried to reciprocate, but seemed unable to. "My name is Eloise. I was married once to a very kind man named Liam, but he passed away a few years ago, and my farm was recently burned to the ground, so I feel a little aimless right now. I have friends out east, and I've been planning to visit them for years. Now that my farm is gone, it's the right time."

Anna lifted the photograph of Liam and Eloise, and her eyes glittered, as though she recognized the power of their union. Eloise wasn't sure their love had been so, so strong, but it had lasted, and that was something.

Anna lifted her eyes to Eloise's, her lower lip quivering. "If you really don't mind."

"It would be the greatest blessing I can think of," Eloise assured her. "Please. Come along."

Anna dropped her head against the booth cushion and closed her eyes. This close-up, she looked every bit a Richards rather than a Copperfield, although Eloise wasn't sure Anna even knew the last name "Richards."

"Do you mind if I go back to the funeral home first?" Anna whispered, barely loud enough for Eloise to hear her. "I'll regret it forever if I don't go."

Eloise squeezed Anna's shoulder. "You take all the time you need, honey. We'll head east when you're ready."

Chapter Six

Anna hated Dean's funeral. She sat in the front row with his parents and his siblings and stared at the floor, listening to a minister who hadn't truly known Dean at all talk about his wonderful personality, his love of baseball, and his achievements in teaching, as though one person could only be made up of a few traits and that was that. But over the past year, Anna had spent real time getting to know the complexities of Dean Carpenter. She'd learned how sensitive he was, how passionate he was about teaching, about how much he hated cinnamon— and about how little he respected his father, who'd cheated on his mother back in 2001 and eventually wormed his way back in.

This was the family Anna had thought she was joining. Now, they looked at her sullenly, as though Anna was a reminder of the life Dean had left them for. If only he hadn't moved to Seattle in the first place. Dean wouldn't have been so reckless in Ohio. Perhaps he would have settled down with his high school sweetheart and lived to be ninety-one.

Regarding the high school sweetheart, Anna met her, too.

Her name was Chelsea, and she was sweet, doe-eyed and could not stop crying about how much she'd loved Dean, even though he'd broken up with her when he'd moved to Seattle. "I used to hate Seattle," she wept to Anna. "I couldn't even look at it on a map." Beside her, Chelsea's husband stood with a curious expression on his face, as though he wasn't sure where to look. For a few seconds, Anna and the husband regarded one another as if they both realized they wanted to be anywhere else but there.

"I have to go," Anna told Dean's high school sweetheart. "Take care of yourself. Okay?" Then, she turned on her heel, walked to Dean's mother, and told her the plan. She said it as though it was the most natural thing in the world— that she had to leave Ohio and that she had to do it immediately. Dean's mother was too distraught to do anything but say, "Yes. You're not family. You don't have to stay for the wake."

Eloise drove a ridiculous truck. When Anna opened the passenger door, she looked up at the seat as though it was the highest branch on a tree. With a huff, she hurled herself into the truck as Eloise laughed gently. She looked at Anna with a lot of generosity and compassion, but without pity, which Anna appreciated.

It was the first time she'd ever hitchhiked. Anna prayed her instincts about Eloise were right.

"How did it go in there?" Eloise asked. She'd changed into a pair of overalls, and she'd removed all of her makeup. It looked as though she'd settled into herself.

Anna groaned. "It was terrible. The minister had no idea what to say about Dean. It felt like he just made stuff up."

"Gosh, I just hate that." Eloise started the engine, and the truck purred around them. "I felt the same way at my husband's funeral. It felt like a formality that had nothing to do with him and everything to do with showing the people in

Muncie, Indiana, that we were good and proper people, the kind of people who did funerals correctly."

"That sounds really hard," Anna whispered.

Eloise flashed Anna a sorrowful look. "Where did you say we can pick up your stuff?"

"It's just five minutes away," Anna explained. "The back door's unlocked, so I can just run in and grab my bag."

Eloise drove out to Dean's family's home, then hovered in the driveway as Anna hurried into the backyard and then through the glass door. Dean's family dog barked at her as she entered, and she took a moment to slide her hand over the soft fur around his ears. Dean had loved his family's dog and shown her a picture of him on their second date.

What would Anna do with all this information about Dean's life now? Where would she store it? Was her brain big enough to keep everything? Right now, she was pretty sure she would never move on from this— that Dean would be the only man she ever loved and that she would maintain that love any way she could. But another part of her hoped that one day, the pain of this would be over. She felt guilty about that.

Eloise drove them eastward from Dayton until nine o'clock that night. Then, she parked outside a Holiday Inn and said, "I'm not very good at driving at night. Do you mind if we sleep here?"

Anna did not mind, of course. She was exhausted, and although she really liked Eloise, she wanted a few hours alone to decompress. In the hotel room, she called her mother, who answered on the first ring, as though she'd been staring at her phone all day, hungry for information.

"Anna," her mother breathed.

"Mom." Anna's face crumpled at the sound of Julia's voice.

"How did it go?"

Anna rolled across her bed and stared at the hotel ceiling. "It was really hard," she answered honestly.

"I can't even imagine."

Anna closed her eyes. "I'm coming to Nantucket."

"I know. I can't wait," Julia said. "Just let me know when, and I'll book the flight for you."

Because Anna had taken an unpaid leave of absence at the travel magazine, Julia had gladly stepped in to assist with cash-flow. Her father had offered to help, as well, but Anna had texted him back to say: "No, thank you."

"I'm actually driving east with a friend," Anna explained. "I had too many panic attacks on the plane."

"Oh, honey." Julia's voice was raspy with worry. "Who is driving you out?"

"You don't know her," Anna said simply. "Her name is Eloise. We stopped at a hotel tonight, but we'll be on the road tomorrow. I'm hoping we'll arrive by the day after that."

"Just be safe," Julia breathed. "I need you here."

Anna closed her eyes, awash with the understanding that Dean's death had reminded her mother of how possible it was that one of her own children could die. Death was always at your door, waiting to happen— to ruin your plans, to destroy your peace of mind.

Anna struggled to sleep that night. Since the accident, it had been non-stop night terrors or else non-stop insomnia, with nothing in between. When six a.m. hit, she showered and made her way to the continental breakfast downstairs to find Eloise already showered and dressed in fresh clothes with a mug of coffee in her hand.

"Wow! You're an early riser," Eloise said.

Anna laughed and poured herself a mug of coffee.

"Ah. I see. You're like me. You're not very good at sleeping," Eloise realized and nodded.

Anna sat beside Eloise, who nibbled through a muffin and watched the televised news.

"How long can you take me?" Anna asked suddenly.

Eloise tilted her head. "What do you mean?"

"I mean, where are you going out east?"

"I can take you all the way there," Eloise said simply. "I haven't been to Nantucket in years."

Anna's eyes widened. "So, you've been to Nantucket before?"

Eloise seemed to weigh something in her mind, as though she wasn't entirely sure what she wanted to say. "I was born on Nantucket."

Anna's jaw dropped. "What are the odds!"

Eloise grimaced and sipped her coffee.

"But you've been living in Indiana?" Anna tried to put the pieces of Eloise's life together based on very brief conversations from yesterday.

"I met Liam out east," Eloise explained. "And he was from Muncie, where his family's farm was. It seemed like a good idea at the time."

"You met Liam in Nantucket?"

"No." Eloise shook her head. "I left Nantucket when I was sixteen."

"That must have been a terrible time to move," Anna said. "Leaving all your friends at sixteen? In the middle of high school?"

Eloise sighed and gave Anna a strange look. "My father was very strict with me. He needed everything to be 'just so.' And when I was sixteen, I messed up very badly in his eyes, and I was sent away."

Anna's jaw dropped. "You were sent away from your family at the age of sixteen?"

Eloise looked unable to finish the story. Her cheeks were the color of paper.

"I'm so sorry that happened to you," Anna breathed. "Did you ever see your family again?"

Eloise shook her head. "I don't want to talk about it," she

said, trying to smile. "It was a long time ago. Suffice it to say, I've missed the ocean. I'm looking forward to walking a few of my favorite beaches again."

Anna allowed them to return to a comfortable silence. On the television screen, a local news anchor spoke in front of a brand-new frozen yogurt shop, which would be opened to the public in time for the beautiful spring day. It all seemed so frivolous after what Eloise had just told her. Anna wondered what it was like to carry the severity of your father's actions so deep into your sixties, as Eloise had. It was suffocating to think about.

Chapter Seven

I t had been a day and a half of driving east. Throughout the journey, Eloise had fallen into a deep and comfortable spell, allowing herself to know Anna, to ask her questions, and to allow Anna to get to know bits and pieces of herself. It had been a long time since Eloise had shown her personality to anyone, especially anyone new, and the result was both terrifying and heart-opening.

At the Hyannis Ferry, Eloise parked outside the ticket office and hurried inside to purchase tickets for both herself and Anna, who slept soundly in the front seat. When Eloise returned to the truck, she tried her best to close the door tenderly, but the truck shook slightly and woke Anna.

"Oh, shoot," Eloise sighed. "I didn't mean to wake you."

Anna rubbed the sleep from her eyes and smeared black makeup across her cheeks.

"I think you really needed to sleep," Eloise said.

Anna groaned and opened the mirror over the top of the seat. "I look rough."

"You don't," Eloise assured her. She reached for her purse

in the backseat and removed a package of Kleenex, which Anna then used to mop up her face.

"How long have I been asleep?" Anna asked.

"Maybe three hours?"

"Really?" Anna's eyes widened, as though the concept of sleeping three hours during a horrific time like this was beyond any comprehension.

Eloise reversed the truck, curved around the office, and got in line behind fifteen other vehicles as they entered the large ferry. After she drove up onto the ramp, a worker in a bright vest directed her this way, then that way, scooping through the beast of a ferry until, finally, she was able to park between two small cars and behind a van.

"Nice driving," Anna complimented her as she opened the passenger door carefully. "This truck doesn't seem like the easiest thing to maneuver."

"I love the power of it," Eloise confessed.

Anna laughed with near joy as they headed up the staircase and toward the cafe on the second story of the ferry, where they purchased coffees and then found a place near the window. Eloise sat, sipped her coffee, and shivered with recognition as a clear memory of being on the ferry with her father came to her. She hadn't considered the memory in years— hadn't remembered that they'd bought ice cream cones and laughed together, father and daughter, so many years before the fateful day he'd kicked her off the island. The memory was sun-dappled and nearly impossible, yet she was one hundred percent sure it was real.

"Where are you staying on the island?" Anna asked suddenly. This brought Eloise from her reverie.

"Oh. I have somewhere," Eloise said with a wave of her hand. This was obviously a lie.

Anna furrowed her brow. "Well, I want to invite you to The Copperfield House tonight for dinner. I insist on it."

Eloise's heart shattered. This was everything she wanted in the world.

"I don't think so, Anna," Eloise said tenderly.

"I won't take no for an answer. You'd love it there, anyway. It's this beautiful Victorian home that my grandparents purchased back in the seventies and ultimately transformed into an artist residency. For many years, artists from all backgrounds came to the residency to make music, films, books, and paintings."

"It sounds so magical," Eloise whispered, as though this was the first time she'd ever heard of the place. In actuality, she knew just about everything there was to know about The Copperfield House. She'd even watched the documentary that a previous resident had made about the place. She'd cried the entire time.

"And my grandmother is an incredible cook," Anna continued, pushing it. "She spent a few years in Paris, where she learned how to cook French cuisine."

"Your grandmother sounds like an impressive woman," Eloise said, her voice wavering.

"She would love you," Anna assured her. "Everyone would. I mean, you went out of your way to drive me all the way here from Ohio, of all places. They'll welcome you like a member of the family."

Eloise's eyes filled with tears, which she quickly blinked away.

"Say you'll come," Anna urged her.

"I really wish I could," Eloise said. "But I have plans."

Anna shifted back in her chair. For a moment, Eloise thought Anna would pester her and demand what plans, exactly, she had. But instead, Anna said, "Okay, but you're not off the hook, you know. We'll get you to The Copperfield House before you leave Nantucket."

Eloise pressed her lips together and tried to smile, but

couldn't quite manage it. "How long do you think you'll stay on Nantucket?" she asked Anna.

Anna dropped her gaze and stared into her coffee cup. "I don't know. I'm taking a leave of absence from work. Every single corner on every single street in Seattle is filled with memories of Dean, of how we met and fell in love. How can I just go back to that like nothing happened?"

Eloise nodded, as she understood better than most. Every room of the farmhouse had been filled with memories of Liam, and they'd initially cut her to the core. She hadn't ever dreamed the house would burn down, that the memories would become ash that ultimately floated into the ether, along the fields, and out into the open blue.

"I thought Seattle was my future," Anna said. "And now..."

"There's no rush, honey," Eloise assured her. "You need to be patient with yourself. You need the comforts of home."

* * *

Eloise hugged Anna goodbye on the ferry and watched as she traced the path down the staircase and out into the April sunlight. In the distance, three women flailed their arms next to a waiting vehicle, and Anna jumped up and waved back. Eloise's heart lifted with the knowledge that soon, Anna would be safe within the arms of the Copperfield Family. She'd done a good thing in taking her home.

Eloise returned to the truck and waited quietly as the cars in front of her disappeared down the ramp and gave her space to move. As she drove down the ramp and out onto the street, her heart leaped into her throat, and she was overcome with the realization that this was Nantucket. This was the island she'd once called home.

Eloise rolled down her truck window and inhaled the salty air as tears came to her eyes. *How was it possible it had been fifty years since she'd seen this gorgeous place?* Overwhelmed, she pulled into a nearby parking lot, where she parked and felt tears rain down her cheeks. Along the nearest sidewalk, a young mother corralled three children, all in brightly colored spring jackets, with ice cream cones in their hands. Behind them, lovers young and old walked hand-in-hand, their hair caught in the Nantucket winds.

Eloise thrust herself from the driver's seat and leaned against Liam's truck, lifting her face toward the sun. For the first time in a very long time, she felt that her father had robbed her of a wonderful life— that he'd ripped the life that was meant to be hers out from under her and forced her to make something out of nothing. It felt unfair.

Still, Eloise didn't want to be the type to carry that anger around with her, not this long after what had happened. Anger festered. It caused wrinkles. It destroyed your heart.

Eloise got back into her truck and routed herself toward a hotel she'd once been very impressed by— one where tourists who sailed and dressed up for dinner stayed. Eloise parked in the parking lot and walked into the lobby with her overalls still on, past vacationers in sleek pantsuits and Italian-cut suits. Her money was just as good as their money, even if she didn't wear it.

"Hello, and welcome to the Garden Bay Hotel," the woman at the front desk greeted her warmly, as though she was just another tourist.

"Hi," Eloise said. "I would like to book a room."

"How long?" The woman placed her fingers on the keyboard and began to type quickly.

"Three weeks," Eloise heard herself say.

"Wonderful," the woman said. "Normally, we don't have rooms available for such a long time, but it's only April. You're in luck."

"Wonderful," Eloise said.

"I assume you're here for the Daffodil Festival?"

Eloise's heart opened at the thought. "Yes," she said. "I just adore the festival."

"Me too." The woman smiled. "All those glorious blooms everywhere make me forget winter altogether, I think. They're healing for the soul."

Eloise took the hotel key card with her, went out to her truck to grab her suitcase, and then boarded the elevator to the third floor. Her room had a queen bed and a window overlooking the street, and in the distance over the tops of houses was the gleaming bay, which was just as crystal-clear as it had been in Eloise's dreams.

For a little while, Eloise collapsed on the bed and stared at the ceiling, wondering at the immensity of life. *How was it possible she was there? How was it possible she'd just spent so much time with Anna Crawford?* A part of her feared she would wake up in a few hours in her bed in Indiana, perhaps even in the farmhouse, as though none of the past week had happened at all. *What would she do, then?*

Eloise cleaned herself up, donned her overalls again, and returned to her truck. She watched herself drive the route, as though she was far above her truck and not in the driver's seat, until she parked in the cemetery parking lot. There, she slipped out and entered the gates, where she froze, suddenly terrified. Many years ago, she'd been at the cemetery to bury her grandmother, who'd passed away when she'd been only a girl. She remembered her itchy black dress and that her mother had curled her hair. She remembered that her shoes had been too tight, that it had hurt to walk through the rows of gravestones.

It took Eloise longer than she'd expected to find them. But soon, there they were: April and Keith Richards, her dearly beloved parents. It was surreal to see their names etched within the gravestones, along with the dates of their births and deaths, and even more surreal to realize that a part of her had half-expected they'd still be here on Nantucket, waiting for her to return. But that wasn't the case. In the past fifty years, both of her parents had passed on— her father with his dark and angry heart, and her mother just going along with whatever her father said.

Eloise collapsed in front of their graves with her heart in her throat. With her finger, she traced first her mother's name, then her father's, as tears rained down her cheeks.

"I know you didn't know what to do with me," Eloise finally said, her voice breaking. "I didn't know what to do with me, either. I still don't."

Exhausted, Eloise stretched out on the grass in front of her mother and father's graves. The grass was new, fresh, and springlike, so she inhaled the beauty of it as her spirit lifted to the air above them. Someone had planted flowers in front of their graves recently, and the flowers flourished in yellows, reds, and oranges and filled the air with vibrant life.

It was here, lying in the grass beside her parents' graves, that she reached the depths of forgiveness. She could do nothing but love who they'd been and the goodness they'd given her when they'd been able to— and forget the darkness they'd brought to her life.

Maybe she should have reached out to them as an older woman. Maybe she should have invited them to her wedding or asked if she and Liam could come to visit. Maybe she was partially to blame for the very long silence, which had only intensified with their deaths.

Chapter Eight

Anna and Julie laid back on the bed that would be Anna's during her stay, both staring at the ceiling. Despite her three hours of sleep in Eloise's truck, Anna was exhausted, her eyes bleary. Julia's face was marred with worry.

"He just disappeared," Anna whispered, not for the first time to her mother. "Out of thin air. Just like that."

Julia reached for Anna's hand and held it tenderly. "I can't imagine what that felt like. It's one of the worst things I can imagine."

Anna swallowed the lump in her throat. Around them, The Copperfield House sighed and creaked with the springtime winds.

"I'm just so glad to be here," Anna said. "I wasn't sure how I was going to make it."

"Your friend Eloise is still on the island?" Julia asked.

"I asked her to come to dinner," Anna explained. "But she had plans."

Julia was quiet for a moment. She then propped herself up

on her hand and regarded her daughter with sharp eyes. "I contacted a grief therapist here on Nantucket just for information about what she could offer you. Would you consider going?"

Anna considered the massive weight on her chest, which seemed to press at her lungs and crack her ribs and make her heart bleed. "I don't know if it would help."

"Don't you think it's worth a try?" her mother asked.

Anna lifted her torso and let her legs hang over the side of the bed.

"Just think about it, honey," Julia urged her. "Your father said—"

Anna turned and gave her mother a dark look, one that made Julia stop speaking. "You've been talking to Dad?"

"Honey, we're worried about you," Julia breathed. "Our problems are minuscule compared to yours."

"I just hope he knows he can't just slink back into our family like that," Anna said softly. "He wanted out, and now, he's out."

"Honey..." Julia placed her hand on Anna's upper back and rubbed it, but she didn't say anything else.

A moment later, there was a knock at the door. Julia and Anna called, "Come in," and Scarlet appeared in the crack, a half-smile on her lips. Scarlet was Anna's cousin, and she'd just moved to the island full-time in the wake of her mother's cancer treatments and a big breakup back in New York City. Anna didn't know her well, but she seemed to be a sweetheart.

"Grandma says dinner is almost ready," Scarlet explained.

"She sent you to get us?" Julia asked with a funny laugh.

"Grandma runs this house," Scarlet said, matter a fact. "Everyone knows that."

Julia eyed Anna knowingly. "I don't blame you if you don't want to come down."

"No, no. I want to see everyone." Anna brought her hair up

into a ponytail and reached for a sweatshirt, which she shrugged over her shoulder. She then followed after Scarlet, with Julia hot on her heels, down the circular staircase and all the way to the kitchen, where Greta Copperfield stood in all her glory at the stovetop in a beautiful apron.

Immediately, Greta placed her spatula to the side and hurried over to Anna for a bearhug. Anna's head fell against her shoulder, and she suppressed a sob.

"It's so good to see you, honey," Greta whispered as she moved back and looked Anna deep in the eyes. "We're so glad you're here."

As usual, the kitchen at The Copperfield House was vibrant with wonderful scents and conversation. Aunt Ella sat at the kitchen table with her son, Danny, who was a senior at Nantucket High School and hard at work on a final paper about economics. Beside him sat Ivy, Scarlet's younger sister, who was a senior doing online classes, as her entire family had moved out to Nantucket a few months before her graduation. Aunt Alana burst into the kitchen at that moment, whipping her large Chanel sunglasses from her eyes as she cried out, "Is that my darling, Anna?"

Anna laughed and allowed herself to be hugged by her beautiful, ex-model aunt, who always smelled of something intoxicating and seemed effervescent and alive. Although her Paris and modeling days were through, she brought a bit of flair to The Copperfield House.

Anna did her best to hug as many of her family members as she could, bouncing from room to room and hearing how everyone was. Everyone greeted her warmly and was careful not to mention how sorry they were about what had happened, as they knew better than anyone not to point at the sight of the injury. It only made it worse.

"Danny, get up, won't you?" Greta swatted Danny's shoulder. "You're done with economics for today, anyway."

Danny laughed and jumped out of his chair, bringing his laptop with him.

"That's for you, Anna." Greta pointed.

Anna did as her grandmother said, perching in the chair at the kitchen table. Greta then hunted through a large jar and produced a chocolate chip cookie, which she placed in front of Anna.

"Nobody else is allowed to destroy their appetite," Greta explained. "Only you. And only today."

Anna laughed and took a delicate bite from the chocolate chip cookie, which immediately melted in her mouth. "They're incredible, Grandma."

Greta returned to the stove and smiled to herself, as though confident that if you just gave someone enough soul-affirming food, they could get through anything.

"Now, Anna. Tell me. Your mother said you traveled here with a girlfriend of yours?"

Anna took another bite of the cookie and considered how to explain the Eloise of it all. "By chance, I met a woman heading to Nantucket."

Greta shot Anna a strange glance. "By chance?"

"I was in Ohio for Dean's funeral," Anna said, her voice skipping at Dean's name. "At a diner, I was having a very hard time, and a woman took pity on me."

"And she was heading to Nantucket?" Greta looked flabbergasted.

"Yes," Anna explained.

"You hitchhiked," Aunt Ella said, snapping her fingers. "I remember those days."

"Don't you dare make her think that's the right way to live," Greta said to Ella.

To this, Aunt Ella winked knowingly, then said, "You shouldn't have done that, Anna." Her smile told Anna she was teasing.

Anna took another bite of chocolate chip cookie as Greta switched her weight at the stovetop. It seemed she'd cooked another Greta Copperfield classic— chicken a la orange. Had Anna not been devastated and very far outside of herself, she might have been hungry for it.

"It doesn't matter now, Grandma," Anna said quietly. "I made it here in one piece."

Greta sighed and took a drink from her water glass. "We've been so worried about you, Anna."

Anna stared at her cookie, not wanting to see the tremendous worry and sorrow across her grandmother's face. Only a few months ago, Grandma Greta had stuffed Dean with French cooking, with cookies and cakes, and he'd laughed about gaining seven pounds on a single trip. "Your grandmother wanted to fatten me up and serve me for Christmas dinner," he'd joked.

"Tell me about this person," Greta said. "The woman who picked you up from some diner in Ohio. What is she doing on Nantucket?"

"She was born here," Anna said.

"Wow." Ella's eyes widened. "That's lucky. Not many people are born here."

"And she's around your age?" Greta asked.

Heat swelled across Anna's cheeks. "She's a bit older than me."

"How much older?" Greta asked.

"I think she said she's sixty-five."

Greta's eyes widened. "You hitchhiked with a sixty-five-year-old woman all the way from Ohio?"

Anna turned to look at Ivy at the kitchen table beside her, but Ivy was focused on her phone and seemed unwilling to save Anna from Greta's barrage of questions. Aunt Alana breezed in and out of the kitchen, fetching wine as she chatted to Julia in the dining room.

"But she hasn't lived here since she was a lot younger," Anna explained. "She's been in Indiana."

"Indiana? Of all the places to end up after Nantucket!" Greta shook her head. "What was she doing there?"

"She married a farmer from Indiana," Anna said. "He died a few years ago. Coincidentally, her farm burnt down on the same day that..." She trailed off, unable to say the unthinkable — that Dean had fallen to his death only days after he'd asked her to marry him. "Anyway, she figured it was a good time to make a pilgrimage east. Lucky me."

"Lucky you," Ella echoed with a soft nod.

Anna did her best to eat as much of dinner as she could. She sat at that enormous dinner table, surrounded by Uncle Quentin, Aunt Catherine, Scarlet, Ivy, James, Aunt Ella, Uncle Will, Danny, her mother, her mother's boyfriend, Charlie, Aunt Alana, Alana's boyfriend, Jeremy, and, of course, Bernard and Greta, and it seemed that everyone had something to say and needed to say it all at once. Anna sat very quietly, sipped a glass of wine, and forced pieces of chicken to her lips. Across from her, Scarlet smiled kindly and nodded in understanding.

After dinner, Scarlet sidled up next to Anna and asked if she wanted to go for a walk along the beach. Anna's heart swelled at the idea. All she wanted in the world was to feel the sharp breeze across her face.

They bundled up in spring jackets and hats and trudged out the porch door, waving goodbye to Uncle Quentin and Bernard, who sat at the porch table. Once on the sand, their feet dipped with each step, and they laughed at the ferocity of the winds. Still, it was better than being cooped inside, where Anna feared her sorrows would form into another panic attack.

"How has it been for you?" Anna asked Scarlet after a little while. "Living here, I mean."

"It's been such a relief," Scarlet answered, her face relaxed. "The city was eating me alive. After Mom's diagnosis, I barely kept myself afloat. Next came the whole Owen debacle, and I thought I was going to go insane."

"I still can't believe that guy."

"Tell me about it," Scarlet said with a sigh. "Dad and I have to go to the city for his hearing soon."

"That'll be hard."

"Yes. It will be. Because a part of me still loves him, you know? I lived with him for a very long time," Scarlet breathed.

A part of Anna screamed with anger for Scarlet; another screamed with sorrow for herself. All she'd wanted was to move in with Dean one day. She'd never even gotten that chance.

After a long walk down the beach, the girls turned to gaze out across the water. Evening light dimmed to blues and grays, and the ocean was silver and glittering with a sort of magic.

Before she could stop herself, Anna heard herself speak.

"I have absolutely no idea what to do with myself."

Scarlet nodded. "Nobody is asking you to do anything."

"But just recently, I was demanding so much of myself," Anna rasped. "I had just gotten a new job and a new, crummy apartment. My boyfriend had just asked me to marry him, and I'd accepted. My life was going somewhere. And now?"

"Now, you're on Nantucket," Scarlet finished. "With a family who loves you. We'll help you through this, Anna."

Anna's stomach twisted. She wasn't entirely sure she could be "helped through" anything, let alone something as traumatic as this.

"Mom wants me to go to a grief therapist."

"You don't want to go?" Scarlet cocked an eyebrow.

"I guess I should," Anna said. "It just makes it all the more real, you know? A part of me thinks I'll wake up tomorrow in that terrible apartment in Seattle and go get brunch with Dean. Another part of me knows that life is dead."

Scarlet placed her hand on Anna's upper arm as another gust of wind threatened to rip them apart. "I can't say that everything will be all right because I know that's not true. Not after what you've been through. I just want you to know that if you need to talk to anyone, or vent to anyone, or just sit by anyone without speaking, I'm here."

Anna was wordless. For a moment, she locked eyes with Scarlet, then bowed her head and allowed several tears to fall.

Scarlet was right about many things— that Anna was surrounded by family and love. She supposed she was luckier than most on their darkest days, but it still didn't take away the harshness of the pain.

Chapter Nine

Eloise spent the first night on Nantucket in lonely bliss. She walked the streets in her overalls, gazing at the colonial architecture, reliving old memories and people-watching, wondering how many of the men and women she saw had been on the island back in the sixties and seventies when she had been. Probably not many.

Eloise grabbed a circular table at a little Italian restaurant and ordered herself a glass of merlot and a plate of spaghetti with truffle oil, which she ate slowly, savoring every bite. Around her, men and women were dressed up immaculately, enjoying one another and the beauty of themselves. Eloise felt she needed no other outfit than her overalls. She was a Nantucket-born, Indiana-bred individual. It was as though she carried the farm around with her.

See, Liam? I really did love that silly farm. I really did love you. She thought this as she twirled spaghetti around and around on her fork, then ate it.

It was regrettable that she'd told Brenda and "the girls" that she'd never thought of Liam as her one true love. *What did that even mean, anyway?* Back when she'd met Liam, he'd been the most handsome and dashing man in her community college, and the fact that he'd chosen her to flirt with out of the other girls in the class had nearly brought her to her knees. She'd married him because she loved him, and that was that. She hoped he'd felt her love till the very end.

It was strange to mourn Liam this far away from his farm and so many years after his death. She supposed that, with the burning of his farm, Liam had died a second death.

At the table next to Eloise sat a married couple. When the gentleman stood up to use the bathroom, the woman locked eyes with Eloise and smiled. "Hello," she said. "Are you enjoying your dinner?"

Eloise was surprised to be spoken to. "I am! And you?"

"It's delicious," the woman said. "This is our second time in this restaurant. I can't get enough of it."

Eloise smiled and began to turn her attention back to her plate of pasta when the woman spoke a final time.

"You know, I think you're really brave for eating alone at a restaurant like this."

Eloise's ears pricked up. She turned her eyes back to the woman, feeling like the biggest clown in the world. *Did everyone think of her as pitiable?*

"Really!" The woman said it quickly, as though she sensed Eloise was embarrassed. "I've never done it, but I think when I get back home to Connecticut, I'm going to try."

Eloise took a deep breath and decided to let the woman's words flow through her. She raised her wine glass and said, "You really should. I do some of my best thinking when out by myself."

That night, Eloise slept in the Nantucket hotel room better than she'd slept in years. When she woke, it was eight in the morning, and light flooded through the crack in the drapes.

There was a sense of expectation in everything, as though Nantucket had been awaiting her return all these years.

Eloise showered, dressed, and went downstairs for coffee and eggs from the dining room. Afterward, without pausing to think about what it meant and how frightened she should have been about it, she headed outside, walked the half-mile downtown, and entered the Nantucket Records Office, where a woman at the front counter greeted her warmly and asked her how she could help.

"Hi!" Eloise's voice was overly bright. "I'm curious about adoption paperwork from the seventies. Do you have those records here?"

The woman gave Eloise a curious smile, then raised a single finger and placed the phone on the desk to her ear. "Hi, Jeremy. I have a woman up here who needs to speak with you."

A few moments later, a handsome man in his forties appeared at the top of a staircase that led to a basement beneath the record's office. He introduced himself as Jeremy Farley and said he'd been working in the record office for decades. Eloise liked him immediately and thought that perhaps in his teenage years, he'd been the class president or the football captain. There was just something you had to love about him.

Downstairs, Jeremy led Eloise to his desk, where— surprise, surprise, there sat a photograph of Jeremy and a woman who could only be Alana Copperfield. Eloise stared at the gorgeous woman in the picture, with her head flung back so that she could smile up at Jeremy, and realized that nearly every person in the Copperfield Family had found their happily ever after. Nearly everyone except for Anna.

"How can I help you today?" Jeremy asked with a smile.

Eloise's breathing was irregular. *Where was that confidence she'd had earlier?*

"I was hoping to see some adoption paperwork from the seventies," Eloise said. "It would have been 1973."

Jeremy palmed the back of his neck as worry marred his face.

"Uh oh," Eloise tried to joke. "That doesn't look like a good sign."

"Unfortunately, all Nantucket adoptions from that time were closed – and much of that paperwork was lost. We have nothing to indicate who adopted who." He scrunched up his face and added, "I've had a few people coming here for this exact reason over the years. It always breaks my heart to tell them that."

Eloise sighed. "I see."

"The rules changed over the years for just this reason," Jeremy added.

"I'm glad to hear that," Eloise said. "Thank you for your help."

Eloise left the record's office after that and wandered through downtown Nantucket, which had, just that morning, exploded with what seemed to be hundreds of daffodils. Far down the road was the team of planters, and they wheeled large wheelbarrows filled with daffodils and soil.

Eloise stood on a street corner, closed her eyes, and inhaled the intoxicating smell of hundreds of daffodils as her head spun with wonder. There was no record of what had happened— nothing to prove she'd lived through that fateful day.

Maybe that was okay. Maybe Eloise had never been meant to know.

Eloise wandered through the streets and eventually found herself in front of a cute coffee shop, where she purchased a cappuccino and something called a "Daffodil Lemon-Ginger Muffin," which was specially made for the Daffodil Festival. She sat in the splendor of the sun outside the coffee shop and ate the muffin slowly, engaging with its unique flavors.

Perhaps this was how she could live out the rest of her days —alone yet relishing the beauty of her surroundings. Perhaps that was all she could hope for.

After Eloise finished her cappuccino and muffin, she began to walk back to the hotel for a late-morning nap. Perhaps after lunch, she would drive out to the other side of the island and walk the beaches she'd once known, the ones where her mother had taken her for picnics.

"Excuse me? Would you like a daffodil?"

Eloise turned to find a teenage girl before her with her arm extended to hand Eloise a daffodil. Eloise blinked at the gorgeous flower, then again at the girl, unsure if either thing was real. "Goodness," she breathed.

"You should take it," the teenager said. "We want everyone to have a little piece of the festival."

Eloise thanked the teenager, then held the daffodil against her chest as tears sprung to her eyes.

"Do you mind if I take your photograph?" the teenage girl asked.

Eloise lifted her head to gaze at the teenager, who'd brought a large camera to her eyes. Before the flash, Eloise felt her lips curve into a smile. This was the first photograph anyone had taken of her in years, and she didn't plan to mess it up.

"Thank you," the teenager said. "You look beautiful with your flower."

Eloise knew the teenage girl didn't truly mean that— that to her, Eloise looked like a wrinkled old prune. Still, she appreciated the sentiment, thanked the girl, and turned back toward her hotel. As she went, there was a skip to her step, because the fact that she'd been seen and even photographed meant something more to her than most people.

No, she hadn't managed to find anything at the record office. But perhaps, in coming to Nantucket Island, she'd only been looking for herself.

Chapter Ten

For Anna, the days were long and grueling. One entire day, she didn't bother to leave her bedroom except to fetch a small bowl of oatmeal, which she barely choked down. Her family was worried about her. Scarlet had brought her snacks, and Julia checked on her hourly. But the fact of it was, sometimes, Anna just needed to fall into bed and allow herself to feel the depths of her sorrow. She supposed this was what grieving was.

Three mornings after her arrival, Anna rolled out of bed and forced herself to get a cup of coffee downstairs. There, she found only her Grandpa Bernard at the kitchen table, a mug of coffee to his left and an entire newspaper spread out before him.

"Anna!" Bernard's smile was generous and warm. "Good morning." Very spry for a seventy-something, he sprung up to fetch her a mug of coffee, which Anna thanked him for. "Don't worry at all. Sit down, will you?" He gestured toward the chair beside him, and Anna fell into it, grateful, for once, not to be alone.

"Your grandmother always writes better in the mornings," Bernard explained. "She made breakfast for the high schoolers this morning, and then, she retreated to her office. I suppose I won't see her till afternoon."

"And you work better at night?" Anna asked, remembering what her mother had said.

"I suppose so," Bernard said. "But I've been a bit lazy about writing lately."

Anna knew his laziness stemmed from his newly rediscovered love affair with her grandmother. Last December, he'd had to run off to Paris to make her fall back in love with him— a story that, to this day, nobody in the Copperfield Family knew the extent of. *What had happened in Paris?*

"I hope you've been comfortable here?" Bernard asked.

"Very," Anna said softly. "I can't imagine a better place to be right now."

Bernard lifted his mug of coffee and sipped it, his eyebrows dropping over his eyes. For a moment, Anna allowed herself to consider the twenty-five years this man had spent in prison. *How had he spent his days? Had he had friends in prison? What had he thought about every single day to get him through?*

"You're a writer, Anna. Like me. Like your grandmother. And like your mother," Bernard said then, surprising Anna. Anna hadn't known her grandfather knew much about her career or her future goals.

"I guess. But I'm more of a travel writer. Or, I thought I wanted to be one."

Bernard's look darkened. "I read the two articles you've written so far," he said. "They're stupendous. They have such personality, and they sizzle with life and color. That requires a unique talent. It's not to say I think you 'got it genetically' from your grandmother and I. Rather, I believe it's entirely your own. Kudos."

Anna's cheeks were warm with embarrassment. She had no idea what to say.

"I don't suppose you've tried to write during this difficult time?" Bernard asked.

Anna shook her head ever-so-slightly. The idea of raising a pen to the paper or clicking away at her keyboard terrified her. A different version of Anna had written. This was the "new" version, the one who didn't know anything at all.

"It took me a little while to write again in prison," Bernard said. "But once I began, I realized it was the only logical way to process my emotions surrounding the trial and the loss of my family. Truly, if you're a writer, there really is no other way."

Anna bent her head in understanding, unsure of how to explain to him that she was broken inside. He, too, had been broken. Probably, he still was in a lot of ways.

Bernard flipped the page of the newspaper to the Local News section and clucked his tongue. "Another Daffodil Festival," he said as he gestured toward the page. "The town is almost too perfumed. You can't get a breath of salty air at all because there are daffodils everywhere."

Anna tilted her head to peer at the newspaper, which spoke about the upcoming events surrounding the Daffodil Festival, including a parade with antique vehicles. Already, she had a sense she would be locked in her room whatever day that occurred, nursing her wounds.

But then, she saw something surprising.

"Can I see that photograph?" Anna pointed to the right-hand page of the newspaper, where a picture of a woman in full color stood in downtown Nantucket with a daffodil in her hands. Even from upside down, Anna could see that the woman wore a pair of aged overalls and that her gray locks were wild, untamed, and impossibly beautiful.

Bernard shifted the newspaper to the side so that Anna

could see the photo in full view. Against the darkness in her heart, she managed a smile.

"That's Eloise," Anna said simply. "She drove me here from Ohio."

Bernard laughed. "No kidding?" He adjusted his glasses on the bridge of his nose and peered down at the small print, where he read, "It just says, 'A Nantucket tourist enjoys the early days of the Nantucket Daffodil Festival.'"

"I suppose that's true, in a way. Although Eloise was born on Nantucket," Anna explained. "I spent a few days with her, but I never thought to take her phone number."

"Grief does funny things to memory," Bernard said simply. "Maybe you can track her down. Will she be on the island long?"

"I don't know," Anna said. "She's a woman of many mysteries."

"Sounds interesting," Bernard said. "It's rare that we have many mysteries here on Nantucket."

"What mysteries?" Greta's voice streamed through the hall-ways and entered the kitchen, and a moment later, the rest of her came with it— smiling, red-cheeked, and carrying several empty mugs, which she'd procured from her writing desk.

"Morning, Grandma! How's the writing going?" Anna brightened her voice as much as she could, grateful to sound a bit more like herself.

"Not bad. Not particularly good, either." Greta placed the mugs next to the kitchen sink and eyed Bernard, Anna, and the newspaper in front of them. "Now, what mystery are you two solving? Is this a Sherlock Holmes and Watson situation?"

"If it is, I'd reckon that Anna is the Holmes in this situation, and I'm only a Watson," Bernard said.

Anna gestured vaguely toward the photograph. "The woman who drove me out to Nantucket is in the newspaper."

Greta's face lost its curiosity, but she did step toward the paper to peer at the photograph. A split-second later, she lurched as close as she could to it, staring at the face as though it would jump out and bite her.

"What did you say your friend's name was again?" Greta sounded breathless.

"Eloise," Anna said simply.

Greta lifted her chin and gaped at Anna, flabbergasted. "Eloise? Eloise from Indiana?"

"But she was born here," Anna reminded Greta. Her heart skipped a beat at the ferocity in Greta's eyes. "Did you know her before she left? I think she's about five years younger than you, so I figured it wasn't likely."

Greta turned toward the kitchen counter and placed her hand over her mouth. She looked on the verge of falling apart. Panicked, Anna hurried to her feet and placed her hand on Greta's shoulder. Something was very, very wrong. Greta gasped for breath, and then she dropped her hand from her mouth and whispered, "Do you know how to get a hold of her?"

Anna shook her head. "No. I didn't get her number."

"Do you know where she's staying, then?"

Anna winced. This was clearly a life-or-death situation for Greta. Why hadn't she thought to get any relevant information from Eloise? Then again, she couldn't have anticipated this.

"She said she had a place somewhere," Anna explained. "I didn't pry."

Finally, Greta raised her chin so that Anna could see her blotchy red eyes. Her lower lip quivered slightly as she said, "Will you help me find her?"

"Grandma, who is Eloise?" Anna stuttered.

Several tears rolled from Greta's eyes. Anna's heart broke with each of them.

"Just tell me you'll help me," Greta breathed. "Tell me we'll find her before it's too late."

Anna squeezed Greta's hand, for once grateful that she could comfort someone else rather than receiving all the comforting. She didn't understand what Greta was so upset about, but it was clearly enormous, the sort of thing she couldn't carry alone.

"I have nothing else to do but help you," Anna said. "Let's get started right away."

Anna gathered the newspaper article that Eloise was pictured in, and together, she and Greta walked to the public library to make photocopies. Throughout the walk, Greta muttered to herself incoherently, and Anna burned with a mix of curiosity and fear. The April sunlight was a little too warm, and she began to sweat beneath her spring jacket. Around them, the air was, indeed, filled with the scent of daffodils, serving as a reminder of how many days Anna had missed from "real life" as she'd huddled inside, hiding away.

Anna sat at the library computer with her hand on the mouse and peered up at her grandmother. "How many copies do you want to make?"

"I don't know." Greta cupped her chin with both hands. "Twenty? One hundred? Anna, I just really don't know!" Her voice was at a higher pitch than Anna had ever heard it.

That minute, Anna's mother texted:

> JULIA: My dad mentioned there's something going on with my mom. That she saw something in the newspaper about this woman named Eloise?

69

JULIA: Can you text me when you understand what's happening?

JULIA: We're all worried here at home.

Anna wrote back quickly to say that she was monitoring the situation, but that Greta still hadn't revealed why this had torn her apart.

"Let's do two hundred," Anna tried, typing the relevant number into the print box. "And let's put your phone number on it."

"Along with the words: **CALL ME - GRETA**," Grandma Greta said.

Anna was careful to type the correct phone number beneath the photograph, along with the words Greta had instructed.

"We can plaster them up all over town," Anna said as she sent the photo and the instructions to the nearby printer. Next came the roar of the printer as it burst to life and began to spit copies into the little ledge beside it.

"And you think she'll see them?" Greta asked, sounding very young and naive.

"I don't see why not," Anna said. "If someone plastered my photograph all over town, I'm sure I'd notice it."

Two-hundred copies of Eloise's beautiful face were printed to the tune of eight dollars and fifty cents, which Greta paid with a crinkled ten-dollar bill. After that, Anna and Greta hurried into the beautiful late-morning and began to tape the pages across telephone poles, beneath shop signs, at bus stops, near the ferry, and on bulletin boards in every coffee shop and restaurant. They also passed out copies to coffee shop baristas, hotel managers, and anyone else they could think of, each time saying the same thing: "We're looking for this woman. Could you call this number if you see any sign of her?"

After nearly three hours of chaotically circling bars, coffee shops, restaurants, and hotels, Greta staggered to a halt in front of a bench near the harbor and collapsed. Her face was slack, and she looked very fatigued, as though the weight of the world was on her shoulders. There was so much Anna didn't understand.

"Grandma?" Anna said softly as she sat beside her and took her hand. "Are you all right?"

Greta shook her head, and her eyes were far away, searching along the furthest horizon. "I don't know how to tell you this. You'll probably think I'm the most selfish woman in the world."

"I would never think that," Anna said. "Because it's not true."

Greta shot her a look, but then continued. "When I left for Paris, I was twenty years old with eyes the size of saucers. All I wanted in the world was to become someone— someone with meaning and purpose and artistry. This was a rare thing for a woman in those days to want.

"For reasons I'll never understand, I was beloved by my parents. To them, I could do no wrong. I think they always wanted a son, someone to hang their hopes and dreams upon, and when they didn't get a son, they decided I was the best they were going to get. My father treated me like an intellectual, and when I said I wanted to go to the Sorbonne, he made it possible for me to get there."

Anna remained very quiet. She'd never been privy to such a personal insight into Greta's past, and it thrilled and mystified her.

"When I left for Paris, my little sister was fifteen," Greta continued. "She was young and funny and adventurous, a girl with her heart on her sleeve. For some reason, my parents were often very hard on her. Her grades weren't as good as mine, and she got into trouble here and there— but no more than any other teenager. I told her to keep her head down, to not get in Mom and Dad's way, but apparently..." Greta trailed off.

Anna's heart had begun to thud like thunder. For the first time since she'd met Eloise, she'd allowed herself to notice small details in Greta's face— details that seemed to belong to Eloise as well. The slant of their nose was the same, as was the way they leaned their head as they thought about something. *Why hadn't she noticed this before? Had the grief put her so deep underwater that she hadn't seen anything around her?*

"Well, apparently, Eloise got herself into one mess or another," Greta continued, her voice breaking. "Because when Bernard and I returned from Paris a couple of years later, when I was pregnant with Quentin, Eloise was no longer in Nantucket."

"Eloise," Anna repeated her name, her eyes filling with tears. "She said she did something when she was sixteen. Something her father kicked her off the island for."

Greta placed her hands over her eyes and sighed deeply. "My parents never told me what happened. They said that Eloise had had to be sent away, and that was that. I pried, of course. I asked where she'd gone. But my father was difficult about it; he put up a very thick wall. And by that time, I was pregnant, and Bernard and I were in the process of purchasing The Copperfield House."

"And Eloise was forgotten," Anna breathed.

Greta bit her lower lip. "I asked several more times that year, I think. Father always said something vague like, 'If Eloise proves to us that she's ready to come back, she can come back.' I never had an address to mail any letters to her. I never knew what to do to reach out. And I suppose, eventually, I let myself believe that what my parents were saying was true. My parents had always been tremendously kind to me— they'd never led me astray."

Anna stared into the distance, trying to wrap her mind around this very old story.

"But how on earth did I run into your sister, of all people, in that diner in Ohio?" Anna demanded, her voice a rasp.

Greta turned to lock eyes with Anna, her face petrified. "I don't know. There's so much I don't know about Eloise Richards. But I suppose, more than fifty years later, it's time I figure her out."

Chapter Eleven

Later that afternoon, Anna had her first appointment with her grief therapist. She dropped off her grandmother back at The Copperfield House, told Julia what she'd learned so far, and then rushed out the door, not one to be late for her very first appointment with her therapist. When she reached the clinic, she waited in the waiting room for only one minute before she was called in, at which point she sat in the chair across from the grief therapist, placed her face in her hands, and burst into tears.

"I'm sorry." Anna half-laughed, half-cried at herself. "It's been a really crazy day."

The grief therapist grabbed a box of Kleenex and passed it over to Anna, who took a tissue and cleaned herself up. "Don't worry about it," she said. "This is a safe space."

Anna blinked through tears to assess the therapist, who seemed only about ten years older than she was and several inches shorter. "I'll try to clean myself up," Anna said as her breathing calmed. "I really do want to have a successful session."

The therapist smiled and said, "There's no such thing as a successful session or an unsuccessful session. We're just here to get to know each other today. The work can take as long as it needs to."

Anna nodded and thanked her.

"My name is Andrea. I've been a practicing grief therapist for six years. To give a bit of context— maybe it's important for you to know that I lost my mother when I was twelve, and I struggled with that loss for many, many years. In fact, even at the age of thirty-two, I still struggle with it. But because of my own grief therapist, I learned tools and skills to help me get through each day until now. I still use those tools."

This intrigued Anna. Was it possible a therapist could just give you tools to survive, tools that acted as coping mechanisms to help you heal and live your life in a normal way? It made sense, she supposed. It wasn't like she could cry out all her sorrows to her therapist and immediately be cured.

"You can introduce yourself to me however you want to," Andrea said then.

Anna closed her eyes and considered how she might have introduced herself even two weeks ago— as a travel writer, as the girlfriend of a teacher, as a Seattle resident. None of those things were true now.

"I'm Anna," she said simply. "And not long ago, I lost my fiancé."

Andrea nodded and furrowed her brow. "That sounds very hard."

Anna closed her eyes against the image of Dean falling off the cliff again. "My mom told me that grief therapy was a good idea."

"As I said, I think we can work together to hone toolsets to get you through this time," Andrea said tenderly.

"I just don't always feel like getting out of bed," Anna said, barely audible to herself.

Andrea remained very quiet.

"I just don't really see the point," Anna went on. "I mean, since I graduated from high school, I've been working myself like a dog. I've built a life on my own without anyone's help. And now, it's like that life has kicked me out of it and said, 'You don't deserve happiness, actually. Everyone else does, but not you.'"

Andrea nodded and furrowed her brow. "Tell me about the life you built for yourself."

Anna crossed her ankles and remembered that terrible studio apartment, which she'd thought was "so embarrassing" until now when she missed it yet felt she could never see it again. "I had finally gotten my dream job as a travel writer."

"A travel writer. That sounds wonderful."

"It really was," Anna said. "For my second assignment, I was sent to Orcas Island to write an article about a new restaurant. My boyfriend surprised me in my hotel room with one hundred roses and proposed to me there. In those moments, I thought everything in my life was on the perfect path. Everything was set for me."

Anna sniffed into a Kleenex, her ears echoing with what she'd just said aloud.

"A travel writer," Andrea said after a little while "Tell me about some of your assignments. How do you prepare for a project like that? How do you decide what to ask your subjects?"

Anna forced herself into the "work" area of her mind, which she now felt was a foreign land. "I don't know. I researched everything there was to know about the person I was interviewing. I wanted my questions to be new and inventive if only to surprise the person. I wanted them to think I was going about this article differently than other journalists."

"And it sounds like you were," Andrea suggested.

"I hope so." Anna paused and inhaled deeply, thinking

again about her grandmother, the sorrow and chaos in her eyes as a result of this Eloise situation. None of it made any sense.

"My grandfather suggested that I write down everything I'm feeling right now," Anna continued. "Because I'm a writer, and that's the way writers process things. But the idea of sitting down with a pen and actually writing down what I'm feeling terrifies me."

Andrea nodded. "I can understand that. Have you considered writing about something else instead? I mean, it sounds like your art form was never about turning inward. It was always about the world around you."

Anna stared at the ground in front of her crossed ankles and wondered how much time she had left in this session. It wasn't that she didn't like Andrea— quite the contrary. It was just that she hated all this attention on herself, on her emotions, on her sorrows.

"What about the Daffodil Festival?" Andrea suggested, her eyes alight.

Anna returned her gaze to Andrea. "What do you mean?"

"Why don't you write a travel piece about the Daffodil Festival?" Andrea said. "Not many people outside of the island really know about it, and it's such a spectacular time of year."

Slowly, Anna began to turn the idea over and over again in her mind.

"I know the festival organizer," Andrea went on. "It wouldn't be a problem for me to reach out to her and make the connection."

Anna raised her eyebrows. "Is it ethical for my therapist to help me with my work like this?"

"Ethical? Good question. But I don't see that it's so unethical. I truly believe that writing is one of the tools that will help you in your healing process. And wouldn't my friend, the festival organizer, be an essential part of an article about the Daffodil Festival?"

Anna sighed. "I suppose everyone on Nantucket knows each other, anyway."

"Exactly," Andrea said with a smile. She then reached for a pad of paper on her desk and scribbled an email address down for one Harriet Thornburg, which she then passed to Anna. "Harriet has been in charge of the Daffodil Festival for several years. She's really busy right now, but she always has time to boost the success of the festival. I'm sure she'd be happy to chat."

Anna took the piece of paper and stared at the address, wondering if she had enough power left within her to come up with even one interview question, let alone fifteen.

"If it doesn't happen, it doesn't happen," Andrea assured her. "But you have her contact, just in case the idea calls to you again."

Anna folded the piece of paper and slid it into her jeans pocket. "I'll think about it," she breathed. "But yeah. Like I said before. I can't promise anything. Maybe the writer part of my brain is dead now. Maybe I'll have to go into something else."

"Every avenue is possible," Andrea assured her. "Here in this room, you don't have to put pressure on yourself in any way."

"Thank you," Anna said, grateful to be in the presence of someone who didn't know her, who couldn't feel the depths of her sorrow, and who could only help guide her toward a better path.

Chapter Twelve

Eloise was in her hotel room with the television on. It was just before six in the evening, and she'd spent most of the afternoon locked away, stewing in thoughts. A very strange part of her itched with the desire to get back in her truck and return to Indiana, to that terrible apartment with the rented furniture, and to the few friends she had in the world. Another part of her screamed to stay on Nantucket, a place she'd dreamed of for years and years— if only to see what would happen next.

The thing of it was, she was far too terrified to reach out to Greta.

After Eloise and Greta's father had sent Eloise to live with her Great Aunt Maude, Eloise had never heard from Greta again. Throughout her older teenage years and then into her twenties, Greta never once reached out. Great Aunt Maude hadn't shared any information about Greta, nor about Bernard and their new baby, and Eloise had been left in the dark. This slap in the face had felt like more than enough of a reason to take off for Indiana.

Still, Greta was now the closest family member Eloise had left in the world. If Eloise didn't reach out to Greta now, all would be lost.

A part of her wished she would have reached out to Greta during the decades Greta had spent all alone at The Copperfield House, which she only knew about after an interview with Bernard Copperfield regarding his recent book. In it, Bernard said, *"It breaks my heart that my wife was without the rest of the Copperfields for twenty-five years. We're making up for lost time. You can bet on that."*

There was a knock at the door. Eloise couldn't fathom who it was, and so she remained very still on her bed for a full minute longer until another knock came.

"I'm coming!" Eloise called, then leaped from bed and hurried to the door. There, she opened it to find the young woman who was normally at the front desk of the hotel. In her hands, the young woman held a piece of paper.

"Hello," the hotel employee said with a smile. "You're Eloise Clemmens, correct?"

"I am," Eloise said.

Slowly, the woman turned the piece of paper around. On it was a black and white photocopied print of the photo the teenage girl had taken of Eloise, the one where she carried a daffodil through town like a hippie.

"Isn't this you?" the woman asked.

Eloise's heart was now in her throat. She handed her a photograph with the words scribed along the bottom: **It's Greta. Call me.**

"This photo was in the paper," the woman continued to explain.

Eloise took the photocopied paper and stared at the image of herself, wearing those silly overalls, and marveled that for the first time in decades, her sister had seen her face. And it seemed that her sister had loved that face so much that she'd made photocopies.

"Someone dropped this off at the hotel desk," the woman said, "but there are hundreds up all over town. You can't go anywhere without seeing your face."

Eloise's lips parted with surprise. It all seemed impossible. But the fact of it was that Greta had decided to search for her, which meant that Eloise finally had to step out from her hiding place. It was the only way.

"Can I ask you a question?" Eloise asked.

"Of course."

"Do you know where The Copperfield House is?"

The woman's eyes brightened. "Oh! Is this Greta Copperfield?" She swatted the paper, where it said, "It's Greta. Call me."

"Yes." Eloise smiled.

"I can give you directions," the woman said. "Do you have a pen?"

* * *

Eloise hurried back into her hotel room and looked at herself in the mirror. The image was of a sixty-five-year-old woman with gray hair that spilled wildly across her shoulders. She wore no makeup — but she didn't like makeup anyway, and she was still in that pair of overalls, which was basically her uniform. If she was going to see her sister for the first time in fifty years, this would have to do.

Eloise left the hotel and walked toward the coastline, following the directions the hotel employee had written her. Throughout, she paused to look at the numerous flyers taped to telephone poles and under street signs and every which way, all of which featured her face. For decades, she'd been gone from Nantucket, and now, she was everywhere, as though

Nantucket had missed her so much it couldn't get enough of her.

When Eloise finally reached The Copperfield House, she stopped dead in front of it and gazed at the beautiful Victorian, remembering that, as a girl, she and Greta had adored the house and dreamed of living there. Greta had gotten that wish. More than that, Greta had gotten to live there for decades— and even raise a family and host artists there.

For a long time, Eloise remained on the sidewalk in front of the old house, terrified to go in. From within came the sound of drums and guitar, and Eloise remembered that Greta's youngest daughter, Ella, was a musician. This was something she'd read about all the way back in the late nineties, so long ago now.

Eloise had begun to talk herself out of this. *It was crazy, wasn't it, to try to mend a relationship with her sister after so many years? Twenty years was one thing, but fifty?* It was outside the bounds of reason.

But suddenly, the front door opened, and an old woman appeared on the porch. She wore a long black dress, and her hair was styled and glowing. Her eyes were bright, illuminated with the April sun, and she looked down at Eloise as though she saw a ghost.

"Greta?" Eloise's voice was hardly a rasp, but it somehow floated through the air to reach Greta's ears.

"Eloise?" Greta took a step toward her, then hurried halfway down the porch staircase with more energy than a woman of seventy should have had.

Eloise matched her sister. She was no longer sure of anything— not of her age or of how much time had passed or of why she'd ever been angry at Greta in the first place. All she knew right now was that Greta was before her. Greta was there, and she was coming faster and faster toward her. Suddenly, Greta was standing in front of her, smelling so wonderfully, her eyes heavy with tears. The sisters wrapped their arms around one another as though they were the only two people left on earth— and in a way, they were. The rest of their family was now dead and gone. It was only them.

"Eloise," Greta breathed. "I can't believe it. I can't believe it's you."

Eloise shook in Greta's arms. She couldn't stop herself. Everything was too intense. Some moments, she felt as though she was fifteen again, hugging her sister before she left for Paris. Others, she felt like a sixty-five-year-old hugging a stranger.

Greta stepped back to show her face wet with tears. "Come inside," she said. "Please. Come into my home."

Eloise walked, wordless, alongside her sister, up the steps and into the house. Within, the sound of the drums and the guitar were louder, and several Copperfields were seated across the living room, chatting and drinking wine. It was rare for Eloise to be surrounded by so many people, least of all people she was actually related to.

"Everyone?" Greta announced with a shaking voice. "This is my little sister, Eloise."

Everyone stopped talking immediately. Jaws dropped, and glasses of wine were set down. It suddenly occurred to Eloise that Greta had never told anyone about her. *Was that possible? Had Greta kept her a secret all this time?*

Suddenly, the woman, who could only be Julia, stood from the far chair and hurried to hug her. "Aunt Eloise," she said, her voice a mix of confusion and happiness. "Welcome to The Copperfield House."

Eloise allowed herself to be hugged, first by Julia, then by Alana, then by Quentin's wife, Catherine, and two other young women, Scarlet and Ivy. Eloise was so nervous that she hardly knew what to say.

Eventually, Greta led Eloise to the back porch, where she poured them both glasses of wine and gestured for her to sit.

Eloise shivered as she sat and wrapped her hand around the glass of wine, both petrified and ready for this next step.

Never in her life had she thought this would happen.

"Eloise Richards," Greta breathed. "I have thought about you every single day since I last saw you."

"It's Eloise Clemmens, now," Eloise said with a soft smile.

Greta's eyes widened. "Eloise Clemmens. My goodness."

Eloise swallowed the lump in her throat, then filled her mouth with wine. The wine itself was better than any wine she'd ever had, which spoke to Greta's immaculate taste.

"My husband died," Eloise said softly. "Three years ago."

Greta's eyes darkened. "I'm sorry to hear that." She said it like she meant it.

"He was a good man. Very kind. Gentle. We wanted children, but they never came. We told each other that we were enough, but I'm not entirely sure if that was true."

"What was his name?" Greta asked.

"Liam," Eloise said as her eyes filled with tears. "It's strange. Since I got back to Nantucket, I've mourned Liam more than I've mourned him in the three years since he died. It's like I had to get out of the context of our lives to remember just how dear he was to me."

"I don't think grieving is ever meant to be linear," Greta said.

"I wish I knew what grief was supposed to be," Eloise said. "I wish someone gave you a blueprint on how it was supposed to go."

Greta nodded and extended her hand, which Eloise took. "I know you've been through a great deal of pain here on your own," Eloise said.

"I have." Greta squeezed Eloise's hand harder. "I wish I had known how to reach out to you. I even looked for you, but I suppose by then, you would have been Eloise Clemmens. And

I never would have guessed you'd end up in Indiana, of all places."

Eloise frowned. "You looked for me?"

"Of course," Greta said.

Eloise's eyes filled with tears. *Why hadn't she reached out to Greta?*

"What was it like?" Eloise asked quietly. "All those years here at The Copperfield House?"

Greta placed her tongue against the inside of her cheek and considered this for a long moment. "It was terrible," she answered honestly. "I thought my life was over. The past year has been such a blessing. It all started when Julia decided to come home. And one after another, the rest of our family came back, as well. But they're all older now. They've been through so much. I see the pain in each of my children's eyes, and it makes me ache for them."

"I'm sure they ache for you, too," Eloise said.

Greta shrugged. "It's not the job of children to ache for their parents."

"But they do," Eloise said. "I think they do. I ache for Mother and Father, at least."

Greta dropped her gaze for a moment. It seemed time for them to talk about the elephant in the room.

Finally, Greta seemed to muster the courage to speak.

"Why did he do it?" she whispered. "Why did he send you away?"

Eloise blinked back tears as the realization struck her. Perhaps Greta had never known.

"I know he was never so nice to you," Greta continued. "I know that he could be cruel. But what made him so angry that he never wanted to see you again?"

"He never told you?" Eloise breathed. "Neither of them?"

Greta shook her head. "I asked them several times, but they always said... They said that you did something unforgivable.

And I hate to confess that, eventually, I just decided to believe them."

Eloise nodded, trying yet slightly failing to understand Greta's point of view.

"I can't believe they never told you," Eloise finally managed.

"Never," Greta assured her. "Please. Help me understand, Eloise. Help me understand what happened when I was in Paris. I've never forgiven myself for leaving you like that. I know whatever happened to you, it was wrong."

Eloise sniffed and leaned back in the porch chair. Beside them, the ocean roared with impossible mysticisms, its waves crashing into one another to form a massive cacophony beneath the darkening clouds.

"I always thought I would get old here," Eloise said very quietly. "I always thought, once I got older, you and I would become the best of friends."

Greta's lips parted with surprise and pain. For a long time, the two sisters regarded one another, overwhelmed with the immensity of the moment.

Yet still, Eloise wasn't sure how to tell Greta what had happened, as it was a story she'd never told anyone— not even Liam.

Chapter Thirteen

News that Eloise had visited The Copperfield House traveled quickly up to Anna's bedroom. Scarlet brought it, her eyes manic with information. She sat at the edge of Anna's bed and wrapped her arms around her knees as she said, "I can't believe it. How did this woman find you at that diner? Isn't it too good to be true?"

Anna's soul had darkened. She felt blackened and bruised, especially after speaking so much about Dean at the therapist appointment, and she peered at Scarlet through the shadows of her room and had to force herself not to ask Scarlet to leave.

"All I know is, you should have seen Grandma today while we put up those flyers," Anna said finally. "She looked panicked, as though she had to find Eloise, or she would fall apart."

"So bizarre," Scarlet said with a shake of her head. "Eloise never mentioned anything about Grandma?"

"Nothing," Anna said.

Scarlet sighed and leaned against the wall alongside Anna's bed. "I keep thinking, what if I didn't see Ivy for another fifty years? What would we say to each other? And you, what would you say to Rachel if you didn't see her for so long?"

"I would probably ask her what she did with all of my hair ties," Anna said with a soft smile.

Scarlet laughed gently and crossed her ankles on the bed. A silence settled over them as Scarlet understood that Anna had very little to give her by way of conversation. Anna's heart went out to Scarlet, although she couldn't fully say it aloud. In these moments, as Eloise reunited with Greta downstairs, Anna felt she couldn't possibly fathom the strangeness of the world. *Why did it give so much love and take so much of it away, seemingly at random? Why had Greta and Eloise's father sent Eloise away; what could she have possibly done, at the age of sixteen, that had necessitated him destroying their family?*

Finally, Anna heard herself speak. "What do you know about Grandma's father?"

Scarlet shrugged. "Basically nothing."

"Me neither," Anna said. "Grandma has only ever spoken of her parents fondly. But it sounds like she was the golden child, the one who could do no wrong."

"I feel so grateful that my parents treat Ivy, James, and I equally," Scarlet said quietly. "I mean, Dad and I hardly spoke the past few years, but that was not because he loved me any differently than my siblings. That all came down to my arrogance. My inability to listen to his worries about Owen."

"You can't beat yourself up about that," Anna urged her. "You're on the other side of all of that now."

Scarlet tilted her head thoughtfully. "Have you spoken to your father at all lately?"

"No. I see no reason to." Anna dropped her gaze, feeling her soul drop into her stomach again. "My father loves all of his children equally, yes. But that doesn't mean he loves us enough." Anna was quiet for a moment, then went on. "I used to think Jackson Crawford was the most intelligent and powerful man in the world. I guess many young women think that about their fathers. But when he left our family and my mother like that— just out of the blue, without even bothering to sit down with my mother and have a conversation about their marriage— he showed just how little he respected all of us."

Scarlet grimaced. "I understand. I think you're right to feel the way you do." After another, longer pause, she asked, "Do you think you'll ever find a way to forgive him?"

In truth, Jackson had texted Anna nearly every day since Dean's death. Sometimes, he just texted: "Hi, honey. I love you." Other times, he wrote out more precise apologies about the past, none of which even scratched the surface of Anna's anger.

"I don't know," Anna answered. "I don't want to say one way or the other. I only know how I feel right now."

"And how is that?"

"Like nothing will ever be all right again," Anna confessed. "And I don't know how my father fits into that story in the slightest, so I haven't made any room for him."

* * *

Later that day, after Scarlet had retreated downstairs and left Anna in the silence of her bedroom, Anna pulled up the information her therapist had given her regarding Harriet Thornburg, the woman in charge of the Nantucket Daffodil Festival. Anna bit hard on her lower lip and considered what Andrea had said: that perhaps it was best to get back to old, creative habits as a way to return to herself. It was worth a shot, she supposed.

Anna emailed Harriet with an inquiry, saying that she had connections with various travel magazines across both coastlines and that she would love to meet and chat about all things Daffodil Festival. "I know you're busy," Anna explained toward the end of the email. "But even just thirty minutes could help me illuminate the article."

To Anna's surprise, Harriet wrote back within ten minutes.

Anna,

Thank you for reaching out! I would be happy to chat all things daffodils, Nantucket, and parades. You've caught me at a busy time, but I always have time for the press. You make our festivals more successful every single year.

Why don't we meet a few hours before the parade on Saturday? I have thirty minutes before I have to race off and press "play" on the day's festivities.

Best,

Harriet

Anna was surprised to watch herself type a response back quickly, as though she wasn't as frightened as she felt. As she crafted the email, she sat up straighter on her bed and felt her mind purr with insight— as though this simple email was able to break through the cloud of grief and let a bit of sunshine in. It lasted only a moment, but it was truly invigorating.

On the morning of the Daffodil Festival Parade, Anna woke up early, jumped in the shower, shaved her legs for the first time in days, conditioned her hair, and then stepped out to dry off and change into an outfit worthy of a travel writer's career. As she dried her hair and shimmied a brush through her tangles, she smiled softly at herself, remembering all the other hundreds of times she'd performed this very action long before her heart had ever been broken so profoundly.

Downstairs, Anna poured herself a mug of coffee and chatted with Aunt Ella and Aunt Alana about her upcoming interview, which she'd spent the evening prepping for.

"You seem really prepared," Aunt Ella said. "So many music journalists who interviewed Will and I over the years had no idea who we were. They just made it up as they went along."

"That's crazy. Your band has always been huge," Anna said.

Ella shrugged. "Indie rock isn't for everyone."

"I remember once when Asher was being interviewed for some art magazine in Hong Kong," Alana said, speaking of her ex-husband. "The journalist got his name wrong halfway through, and Asher threw his hat at him. This was before Asher got his hair plugs, so he wore a hat everywhere." Alana wrinkled her nose at the memory of her tortured artist ex, then laughed. "I don't know what to do with all these memories of this horrible man. Do you think I can have them deleted from my memory?"

Aunt Alana shook her head, having gone too far in a separate direction, then said, "Anyway. I assure you that your interview will go well because you're a well-qualified, empathetic human being with many good questions and good things to say. That's that."

Anna couldn't help but smile at the whirling nature of Aunt Alana's mind. "Thank you for saying that," she said. "I think it really helped."

Anna took one of The Copperfield House's bicycles downtown to meet Harriet Thornburg at a little coffee shop that sold lemon bars and brownies in a gleaming glass case. Anna sat with a coffee and a lemon bar and watched the door nervously, counting the seconds. Harriet was late.

But a moment later, a forty-something woman with black hair and dancing blue eyes burst through the door. Her black hair was a stream behind her, and her gait was frantic, as though she'd spent the better part of the morning putting one fire out after the next.

"Anna!" Harriet greeted Anna immediately. "I recognize you from your website. I hope you don't mind that I did a bit of snooping."

Anna stood, immediately warmed by the generosity of this

person. "Thank you for meeting me today."

Harriet waved a hand and then spoke to the woman behind the counter to order a cappuccino and a croissant. She then collapsed on the other side of Anna's table and puffed out her cheeks. "It's been quite a day."

"And it's not even nine-thirty," Anna joked.

Harriet nodded and removed her sunglasses from the top of her head. "All right, Anna. You have my undivided attention for the next..." She then whipped up her wrist to check the time on her watch. "Twenty-eight minutes and twenty-two seconds."

Anna laughed and pulled out her pad of paper, upon which she'd scribed several interview questions. She then waved her phone as she asked, "I hope you don't mind if I record this?"

"Not at all," Harriet said. "Go for it."

Anna pressed RECORD and set up her first several questions, which asked how Harriet had gotten involved in the Nantucket Daffodil Festival, what her goals for the festival were, and so on.

Harriet answered thoughtfully and brightly, saying, "I was born right here in Nantucket, and as far as I'm concerned, it's heaven on earth. Since I was a girl, I've worked to build a better, healthier, and more open community here in Nantucket to ensure that every single member of our community knows how special they are. I know that sounds a bit naive, a bit childish, but I truly believe in it. There's a very good heart at the core of the Nantucket community, one that I see beating very brightly on the day of the Daffodil Festival Parade. Which, as you know, is today." Harriet smiled.

Harriet went on to explain the various functions and activities that surrounded the Nantucket Daffodil Festival, along with the most important vintage cars to watch out for during the festival parade. Although Anna knew, in many ways, that this was a "puff piece," she found herself wrapped up in Harriet's answers, finding depth to the story where many wouldn't have.

More than anything, Anna found that, throughout the interview with Harriet, she hardly thought of her grief once. It was as though she was allowed to transport herself through time and space and become just another travel writer at the beginning of her career rather than a grieving fiancée.

"Anna, Anna, Anna." Harriet sipped her cappuccino toward the end of their interview and laughed gently. "This was such a remarkable pleasure. It's pretty rare that I find myself thinking about the real reasons I got into something like this."

Anna flipped her pad of paper closed and dropped her gaze, embarrassed.

"I read on your website that you just graduated last year," Harriet said as she gathered her purse over her shoulder.

"Yes. Out in Seattle," Anna explained. "But my family lives here on Nantucket, and I'm spending some time with them."

"Like I said before, I see no reason to live anywhere else," Harriet said as she stood up. "But of course, I can imagine the allure of a place like Seattle. Those beautiful mountains!"

Anna's voice skipped as she hurried to say, "Yes. But Harriet, I can't thank you enough for this interview. I can already imagine how the article will come together. I think my editor will be very pleased."

Harriet extended her hand, which Anna shook. "I look forward to reading it, Anna. And I look forward to following along with your career. I hope we run into one another soon."

"Thank you," Anna said. "And I suppose I'll see you later? At the parade, I mean."

Harriet blushed as she paid at the counter for her cappuccino and croissant. "I imagine if you do see me, I'll just be a blur, running from place to place. But I'll try to wave to you as I pass you by."

Chapter Fourteen

The intensity of meeting Greta Richards Copperfield in the flesh had blown Eloise over. Since that first talk on the back porch of The Copperfield House, Eloise had staggered through time and space, unsure how to go on. Twice, she'd seen Greta again— once to visit their parents' graves and another time for coffee in the downstairs lobby of the hotel. But each time, Greta had sobbed, saying how sorry she was that she hadn't known what had happened back in the seventies and that guilt about it was almost too much to bear.

Now, it was the morning of the Daffodil Festival Parade, which Eloise had agreed to attend with Greta and the rest of the Copperfield Family. Eloise donned her overalls and a light pink turtleneck and took stock of herself in the mirror, both terrified and excited about meeting even more of the Copperfield clan and putting herself out in public in their midst. It seemed a given that she would run into someone she knew from the past at the parade. How their eyes looked when they saw her would tell her everything about how she looked and how old she'd gotten. Then again, whoever this faceless person was had probably gotten just as old, too. Eloise needed to lighten up.

Eloise left her hotel room at eleven and padded downstairs to find Greta already in the hotel lobby in front of a cup of coffee. Her hair was curled elegantly, and she wore a pair of cat-eye sunglasses. Always, Greta had been a portrait of fabulousness.

When Greta spotted Eloise on the stairs, she stood quickly and hurried to hug her. "I'm sorry," Greta said with a nervous smile. "You're probably getting sick of all the hugs and apologies."

Eloise shook her head and again felt tears in her eyes. "You don't have to apologize at all. I've told you that. But the hugs? I'll take as many as you're willing to give."

Greta wrapped her arms around her sister once more as, across the lobby, the hotel receptionist smiled warmly.

"Are you two heading to the Nantucket Daffodil Festival?" the receptionist asked.

"It's our first one together in more than fifty years," Greta said as their hug broke.

"My goodness." The receptionist shook her head. In her late twenties or early thirties, it was clear that fifty years was hardly conceivable to her.

Eloise got herself a cup of coffee and sat across from Greta to enjoy a moment of peace before the festivities.

"So, the entire family will be there today?" Eloise asked nervously.

"All of them," Greta affirmed. "And the ones you didn't meet the other day are dying to meet you."

Eloise made a face and sipped her coffee. "I hope Anna isn't too upset with me."

Greta shook her head. "When Anna first got back to Nantucket, all she could do was talk about how 'incredible' the friend who'd driven her to Nantucket was."

"You're kidding! A friend?

"She sees you as a friend," Greta confirmed. "And why wouldn't she? You helped her through a very dark time."

"Yes. I suppose so." She considered this, then added, "But Anna helped me just as much as I helped her."

"Maybe you should tell her that," Greta tried. "If you want to."

Eloise and Greta walked from the hotel to downtown Nantucket, where, apparently, Bernard and Quentin had already staked out a "perfect parade spot." As they walked, Eloise noticed a moment of jealousy rise up within her— jealousy that Greta had a son and a husband to save her a spot on the parade route. But as soon as the feeling came, Eloise blotched it out. It wasn't useful for her.

"I can't believe I've never met your husband," Eloise said.

Greta smiled a romantic smile, her eyes far away. "For many years, it was like we weren't married at all."

"What were you thinking when he was in prison?"

Greta considered this as they waited for a stoplight to change. Around them, tourists walked through the April sunlight. Some of the women wore daffodils in their hair, tucked behind their ears.

"I tried to pretend he wasn't real," Greta answered honestly. "Isn't that terrible? I would never tell him that now."

"It sounds like that was the only way you could survive," Eloise tried. "You had to tell yourself that such happiness didn't exist. I felt the same way when Father first sent me away. For the first month or so, I cried in that uncomfortable bed as Aunt Maude slept in the next room. I couldn't believe my life had taken such a terrible turn! And then, gradually, I taught myself how to live in this new reality."

Greta's frown intensified. She reached for Eloise's hand and squeezed it. "Do you think, as little girls, we ever imagined our lives would be filled with such suffering?"

Eloise dropped her gaze. "I certainly never did. All I remember is sun-dappled picnics on the beach, biking through downtown, and eating ice cream until it melted along my hand."

"Those are my memories, too," Greta breathed. "I never should have left for Paris. I should have stayed here. Maybe I could have convinced Father..."

"Don't," Eloise instructed her. "Don't play that game. What's done is done. And we're here now. Together."

Very soon, a large hand waved from across a downtown street, and Greta and Eloise scurried across to find Bernard, Quentin, Quentin's son, James, and Ella's son, Danny, attempting to take up as much space on the sidewalk as they could. Eloise's heart opened at the sight of Bernard, who she'd read about tremendously— about his books, his prison sentence, and his new innocence after his children had proven he hadn't committed those crimes. She'd even read his recently published book— the one Julia had put her heart and soul into publishing. It had filled her very boring and lonely nights at the farmhouse.

"You must be Eloise," Bernard said, his voice and eyes warm and welcoming. "I can't believe it."

Eloise smiled and extended a hand, but Bernard raised both of his arms and insisted on a hug instead. Eloise allowed it, laughing gently, then stepped back to shake Quentin's hand.

"Quentin, I watched you almost every night on the news," Eloise said.

Quentin's smile was sincere. "Did you know we were related?"

"She knew everything," Greta said.

"I did know," Eloise confessed. "And it was incredible to see all the work you did over the years."

"Thank you," Quentin said quietly. "That means a lot to me. Aunt Eloise? Should I call you that?"

"You can," Eloise said, surprised at how joyful she was at the sound of this new name.

Very soon afterward, other members of the family appeared. Ella and Will came, along with Alana and Jeremy, who remembered Eloise from her trip to the basement of the record office but didn't go on about it, which Eloise was grateful for. Perhaps Jeremy was accustomed to the delicate nature of the records he handled and the fact that people didn't always want to discuss them aloud.

A little later, Ivy, Scarlet, and Anna appeared around the corner. They wore spring dresses beneath their jackets, and their long legs were athletic and gleaming beneath the April sun. Eloise's heart lifted at the sight of Anna, the young woman who'd been her only friend during those lost days on the road. Anna's face reflected her joy at seeing Eloise, as well.

"Eloise, Eloise, Eloise." Anna said her name over and over and then cupped Eloise's elbows, her eyes alight. "You little sneak!"

Eloise's cheeks were warm with embarrassment. "Anna, I'm so sorry I didn't tell you the truth."

Anna tugged Eloise toward a nearby bench where they could speak away from the rest of the Copperfield Family.

"You don't have to apologize," Anna said simply. "I just want to know more. How did you find me? How did you know I was going to be at that diner?" Her eyes burned with curiosity.

Eloise was embarrassed, but she forced herself to speak. "Gosh, Anna. I don't know. I suppose first, I have to tell you that I kept tabs on the Copperfield Family over the years the way some people keep track of soap operas or sports teams. I always knew who all of you were, but I never imagined I'd ever get to meet you. I suppose it came from a fascination with the life I felt I'd not been allowed to live."

Anna nodded as they sat on the bench, her eyes glowing with empathy. "I get that."

"One evening on the news, they spoke about Dean," Eloise continued, her voice breaking at the name of this poor man who'd lost his life. "I read a little bit about what happened online and couldn't help but notice that Dean was from Ohio, not far from where I was living. I told myself not to do it— that it was too crazy. But before I knew what I was doing, I was in my truck, heading to Dayton. I suppose, for me, there was a gravity around you. You were my last link to my sister, and I just..." Eloise trailed off. "But I couldn't go into the funeral home. That was too insane, even for me, a senile old lady. Instead, I drove to the diner to get my bearings and find a way to turn back to Indiana and leave you behind. That's around the time you walked into the diner in the first place."

Anna's eyes widened at the story. "My gosh. What a coincidence."

"You're telling me," Eloise said. "I thought I was dreaming for most of it. Yet, here we are."

"Yet, here we are," Anna echoed.

"I hope you aren't angry with me," Eloise said. "And I hope you don't think I'm some kind of freak. Since I was sixteen years old and sent away, I've developed such a strange relationship with Nantucket Island— and I suppose, in coming here, I'm beginning to learn how to heal."

Anna gripped Eloise's hand. "Is there some way I can help you?"

Eloise shook her head. "No. But I'm here now. I'm here with my sister, and I'm here with you, and I'm meeting the rest of your wonderful family. Maybe one day, I'll even feel a part of that family."

"You are a part of our family," Anna insisted. "It was fate that we met one another the way we did. But you were always supposed to come to Nantucket. I know that in my bones."

Suddenly, in the far distance came the sound of trumpets, trombones, and tubas. Eloise sat pin-straight and peered down the street as, far to the left, Greta called out, "Eloise! Remember, we used to love the marching band!"

Eloise did remember that. All those years ago, even five years younger than Greta, she and Greta had jumped up and down as the marching band had passed them by, screaming out the lyrics of the songs they played. Eloise had always dreamed of learning to play an instrument, but because she'd been sent away, it had never happened for her.

Together, Eloise and Anna walked back to the Copperfield Family. The others had joined, including Charlie, Julia's boyfriend, and Catherine, Quentin's wife. Catherine leaned down to whisper in Eloise's ear to say, "This place is truly remarkable. You grew up here?"

Eloise smiled, feeling proud of her Nantucket birth. "I did. It's so wonderful to be back."

"Greta seems over the moon to have you here," Catherine said.

But already, the marching band was closer, so close that Eloise could hardly make out what the rest of the Copperfields said around her. The drumsticks splattered across the skin of the drums, and the trumpets blared their song to the high heavens. And at that moment, Greta stepped up beside Eloise, strung her fingers through hers, and called out, "This is it, Eloise!"

With that, the marching band turned the corner and tore toward them, bringing Eloise's heart into the twenty-first century of Nantucket life and love. She blinked several times, unable to suppress her tears. This was one of the happiest days of her life.

Chapter Fifteen

The Nantucket Daffodil Festival Parade was forty-five minutes of non-stop excitement. Anna took several moments to watch Eloise enjoying it, feeling as though Eloise was a young woman on the brink of her life rather than a sixty-five-year-old woman making up for lost time. Still, the euphoria was the same.

After the vintage cars passed, followed by the Girl Scout troupe and the Boy Scout troupe, followed by the ballet dancers, the Nantucket Rotary Club, and so many other faces that Anna half-recognized from her times in Nantucket, the parade finally fizzled out. In its wake, Anna hurried up beside Eloise and hugged her, watching as Eloise's smile widened.

"What did you think of that?" Anna asked.

Eloise seemed wordless. She took a handkerchief from the pocket of her overalls and tidied her cheeks, which were wet with tears. "I don't think I've been that excited since I was a girl."

"Hi, Anna!" Scarlet waved from behind Grandma Greta and Eloise, where she stood in conversation with a group of guys in their twenties. It seemed clear from their stances that the men were at least sort of interested in Scarlet, and they peered through the crowd at Anna with similar interest. Anna wanted to roll her eyes.

"There's a tradition on the island," Eloise said suddenly. "Young men and women always celebrate on the beach after the Daffodil Parade. I remember that well."

"I do, too," Greta said, her eyes heavy with nostalgia. "Anna, you really should go. It's a wonderful time to meet others around your age here on the island."

Anna bristled, caught between her desire to run home and hide under her covers and her desire to live, really live, in a way that would make Dean proud. As she paused, thinking, the crowd of parade-goers began to walk past, headed back home or to the numerous restaurants that stretched along the coast or were clustered downtown.

"Of course, we'll have to grab something to eat first," Grandma Greta said. "As a family." She then turned toward Scarlet to remind her of this, and Scarlet nodded and said, "I know, Grandma. I'll go to the party after. Anna, you up for it?"

Anna raised her shoulders, deciding that she would make up her mind about whether or not she went to the party after she got some food in her. Grandma Greta then laced her arm through Bernard's and gestured to the entire clan as she said, "I made a reservation for us at Uncle Andy's Brasserie."

"For all of us?" Julia asked with a laugh. "I wasn't sure any restaurant on this island could accommodate all of us."

"They had better accommodate us," Greta joked.

Anna fell behind many of the Copperfields, stepping in line with Scarlet, Ivy, and Danny, who spoke excitedly about the upcoming party on the beach. It seemed that, after an entire lifetime in New York City, Scarlet, Ivy, and Danny had all taken to the island easily. Anna, who'd been raised in the suburbs of Chicago, prayed that Nantucket would fit like a glove soon.

As they walked toward Uncle Andy's Brasserie, an older man in a pair of jeans and a green button-down bucked out from the crowd and beelined for Eloise. He moved so quickly that he interrupted the stream of the rest of the Copperfields, all of whom struggled to keep up with Greta, who seemed eager to get to dinner.

"Eloise?" The man sounded incredulous.

Eloise stopped short, and the Copperfields walked around her, leaving her to stare at this strange man. Anna stalled slightly, watching them. Further up, Greta, too, stopped, turned back, and stared at the two of them, clearly intrigued.

"Gosh, it's been how many years?" The man continued to stare at Eloise as though she wasn't real.

Eloise switched her weight from foot to foot. "Fifty years, I suppose."

It had come time for Anna to walk around Eloise, to go up ahead and leave her with this man alone. Anna hurried past, trying her best to deduce what the situation was. Further up, she locked eyes with her grandmother, then muttered under her breath, "Grandma, who is that?"

Grandma Greta's eyes were dark. Very quietly, she said, "Eloise used to date him back in high school before she went away."

Anna's eyes widened. She turned back to watch the couple, this new information sizzling in her mind. In her mind's eye, she could just about see them as two teenagers, him handsome and broad-shouldered, and she petite and bright-eyed. *Where had all that time gone?*

"Do you think Eloise is happy to see him again?" Anna asked.

"I think he's her ghost," Greta breathed. She then tapped

Anna's shoulder and said, "Let's keep going, honey. I shouldn't stare."

Anna followed Grandma Greta back into the throng of awaiting Copperfields, many of whom hadn't realized what the holdup was.

"All right. Let's go," Grandma Greta hollered at the group, beckoning for them to follow as they traced the last of the route to Uncle Andy's Brasserie, which sold a mix of French and American cuisine.

The brasserie had put several tables together to ensure that the entire Copperfield clan could sit together. Anna grabbed a seat toward the end, between Scarlet and her mother, and watched Eloise out of the corner of her eye as she appeared and sat near Greta at the far end of the table. Eloise was white as a sheet, as though that man really had been a ghost. When the server came to take her order, she asked for a glass of wine, and she sounded as though she really, really needed it.

"You really should come today," Scarlet urged Anna, interrupting her reverie. "I just met these guys on the island, and they're really cool."

"I really don't want to meet guys," Anna said softly, her eyes still on her menu.

"They aren't creepy guys," Scarlet assured her. "They've shown me a lot of the island so far. Apparently, the Copperfield name is sort of big around here, and they're glad to get to know this next generation. That means us." She wagged her eyebrows playfully.

Anna sighed, genuinely unsure if she had it in her to socialize. Then again, she'd had a wonderful day— she'd interviewed Harriet for a new article, gotten to the bottom of what had happened with Eloise, and spent a delirious hour with her family at a parade. *Why couldn't she cap the day with a nice, normal party?* Perhaps doing nice, normal things was the only way to get through this.

After they ate, Anna, Scarlet, Ivy, James, and Danny said goodbye to their family and struck out for the beach on the other side of the island, where younger islanders frequently gathered for barbecues and beach parties. Throughout the drive, Scarlet, Danny, Ivy, and James laughed together and talked about the previous party they'd attended, when, apparently, Danny had drunk one too many beers and fallen asleep near the bonfire.

"Your mom would kill me if she knew," Scarlet said with a sigh. "But you're almost a high school graduate, which means you're off to college. I think it's important you start to learn how to take care of yourself."

Scarlet then turned a sharp eye to Anna, who sat in the front seat as she drove. "I watch James like a hawk, though. He's only sixteen!"

James sighed from the backseat. "I can't hide anything from her."

Anna felt wrapped up in her cousins' joys and personal stories and soon heard her own laughter filling the air. When they reached the beach, Scarlet stopped the engine and hurried around the back to grab a twelve-pack of beer. Scarlet then led the charge to the beach party, where it looked like thirty to forty young islanders stood around a bonfire as springtime winds ripped into their coats.

"When the sun comes out, Nantucketers don't wait around for the temperature to go up," Scarlet said. "I appreciate their bravery."

A few of the guys Anna had seen chatting with Scarlet earlier waved from the other side of the bonfire. One of them leaped up to help Scarlet take the beers from the container.

"This is my cousin, Anna," Scarlet said with a smile. "I was telling you about her?"

The guy was around Anna's age, maybe a bit older, with a lopsided smile. "Hey! I'm Jack Thornburg."

"Nice to meet you. That last name... Is your mother Harriet?" Anna asked.

Jack laughed. "That's my mom, the queen of the Nantucket Daffodil Festival."

"No way," Anna said. "I just interviewed her this morning."

Jack tilted his head. "Interviewed her? For what?"

Anna blushed, feeling self-conscious about her career—which was hardly off to any grand start. "I work as a travel writer, sometimes," she said. "And I wanted to write a piece about the Nantucket Daffodil Festival."

"Ah. Yeah. Mom mentioned that," Jack said. "She got really nervous over coffee this morning, wondering if she was going to come across dumb."

"She would never come across like that," Anna said.

"I told her that." Jack palmed the back of his neck, then said, "You're new to the island, yeah?"

"Hey, Anna." Scarlet passed her a can of beer, which Anna cracked, not knowing what else to do.

"Yeah. I'm new." Anna sipped her beer and smiled. "But I guess it's an okay place to live? At least for a little while?"

"I was born here," Jack said. "I can't imagine living anywhere else."

"Did you go to college?" Anna asked.

Jack shrugged. "I took online classes. I'm just a semester away from graduating with a degree. But I don't really need it. I work with my grandpa as a fisherman. We take tourists out on the water when they come to the island."

"That sounds dreamy," Anna said. "Maybe I could write a travel article about your grandpa's company next."

Jack laughed appreciatively. "My family will be forever indebted to you."

Despite Anna's hesitance, she found that she genuinely enjoyed the beach party. Jack introduced her to more of his friends, young men and women who'd been raised on the island

and now either worked in tourism or online. They were friendly and bright, and they asked Anna questions about her travel writing as though she was far more advanced than she was. None of them knew anything about Dean, which Anna was grateful for. Normally, back at The Copperfield House, it was like she had "feel bad for me" written on her forehead.

Here, she was just a normal twenty-three-year-old woman, just as she'd been a month ago.

Around nine that night, Anna drove Scarlet, James, Danny, and Ivy back to The Copperfield House. Anna had had just the one beer, many, many hours ago, but Scarlet was bubbly due to the alcohol and telling eight stories at once. Her joy was contagious.

Anna parked the car outside the house, and the Copperfield kids stumbled out and up onto the front porch. Anna was last, locking the door behind her and waving to her cousins as they barreled up the staircase. Internally, she missed her sister and her brother a great deal and wished they could have been there during this time— but she was grateful for these newfound friendships with other family members.

Anna headed to the kitchen to grab a glass of water. When she entered, she was surprised to see Greta at the kitchen table, facing another man who Anna recognized as Eloise's high school ex-boyfriend. The man was clearly stricken. All the color had drained from his cheeks. *What was going on?*

"Hi." Anna frowned and hurried to the sink to pour herself a glass of water, knowing she had to get out of there quickly.

"Did you have a good time?" Grandma Greta's voice was strained.

"Yes." Anna smiled, first at Greta, then at the stranger. "Well. Good night," she said, then hurried out of the kitchen and up the staircase. She knew she wasn't wanted there. Not then.

Chapter Sixteen

It was after midnight, but Eloise was no closer to sleep than she'd been hours before. In fact, she remained fully clothed, pacing the hotel room endlessly with her hands latched behind her back. Over and over again, that face came to her mind— so handsome, his eyes focused on her as he'd said her name for the first time in over fifty years. "Eloise. Eloise. Is it really you?"

Eloise first met Herb when she was thirteen years old. At the time, Greta had been eighteen years old, the golden daughter of the family, and Eloise had had scabbed knees, a propensity for getting in trouble, and a whole lot of passion for sixties rock. Back then, she'd been really, really into The Beatles (back when all of them had still been alive and they'd still been releasing albums), and she'd spent a lot of her time in her bedroom, spinning their records and dancing along. Her father had thought The Beatles were "silly hippies" and that Eloise was wasting her time listening to them rather than putting her brain somewhere more useful, like her homework.

Only Herb had understood The Beatles the way Eloise

had. Together, at the school lunch table, they'd hunched over their lunch pails and discussed the intricacies of each album, unpacking lyrics and trying their best to comprehend the weight of a world-changing band, who seemed, with each release, to alter music forever.

"It's like they're Mozart, Bach, and Chopin all rolled into one," Herb had said once, his tuna sandwich poised near his mouth.

"This is exactly what I think," Eloise had affirmed. "Paul and John are poets sent from the heavens above, and George is just so talented."

"And handsome," Herb had said. "Admit it. You're in love with George."

Eloise had rolled her eyes back into her head, unwilling to admit the truth. And in fact, Herb had just begun to learn how to play the guitar, a fact that thrilled Eloise. Her crush for him had grown so demanding that, oftentimes, Eloise spent all Saturday in her room, listening to Beatles records and writing in her diary about how in love with Herb she truly was.

But Eloise hadn't had a clue how Herb felt about her, not until they were both fifteen— two years after their Beatles' love had brought them together. When Eloise was fifteen, Greta left for Paris and left a Greta-sized hole in her father and mother's hearts. Lucky for Eloise, this meant that they weren't very focused on Eloise's comings and goings. Oftentimes, she left their family home for hours without saying where she was off to, and when she returned, nobody was ever the wiser.

Herb's parents were much kinder than Eloise's parents. His mother often baked cookies for Herb and Eloise, took them to movies, and drove them out to the beach. She sat at a distance from them with a book, allowing them the beauty of a kind of privacy, and didn't even glance up when they had their first kiss (or so Eloise thought).

When Herb first told Eloise his feelings for her, Eloise

hadn't known how to react. Her love for him seemed just as powerful as any Beatles' love songs, and yet, she wasn't sure how to return his love with words and actions. *Was she supposed to hold his hand now? Were they supposed to tell people they were going steady?*

But because Herb was also her best friend and the nearest person to her heart, Eloise found herself expressing her insecurities, only to have him verbalize his own.

"Let's just make it up as we go along," Herb suggested.

"What if we get it wrong?" Eloise asked.

"I don't think we will." Herb had slipped his fingers through hers and tugged her into him, then kissed her there along the rocks as the ocean lapped up along the sands. Overhead, sunshine unfurled itself from the thick clouds, and Eloise thought, at this moment, that everything would be perfect for the rest of her life.

She'd obviously been very wrong.

Oh, but to see Herb again had taken her deep into the past, far before the days when she'd met Liam and even before she'd had to live with Aunt Maude. After she'd first left the island, she'd dreamed of Herb endlessly and yearned to reach out to him, but her father, her mother, and Aunt Maude had forbidden it, so much so that Eloise was terrified to call. Her parents had already been on the fence about loving her at all— she didn't want to push it.

In her mind, if she paid attention to the rules and showed her parents how good she could be, they would eventually allow her to return. She'd been wrong.

Eloise sat at the edge of her bed in the hotel room and stared into the black night. Clouds had formed overhead, and there were no stars. She reached for the remote control and turned on the local television station, which showed *Pretty Woman*, a film from back in the days when Julia Roberts had still been young. Unfortunately, by then, Eloise had already given up on many of her hopes and dreams. Children hadn't come.

Eloise burned with thousands of questions, all of which she wanted to ask Herb. *But how could she possibly get up the nerve to ask them?* She'd left almost fifty years ago, and Herb had clearly lived an entire life without her.

No— she hadn't seen a wedding ring. That was true. But that didn't mean anything. Sometimes, men didn't wear wedding rings for comfort reasons. Then again, Herb didn't seem like the kind of man who would refuse to wear his wedding ring, as he was the sort of man who appreciated symbols and upheld them.

As the night ticked toward dawn, Eloise began to stew in personal resentment. Again, she questioned why she'd had to come to Nantucket and stir up so much drama. She wasn't a dramatic person in the least. Back in Indiana, she'd been the friend who stopped fights before they started. Whenever she and Liam had begun an argument, she'd sat calmly, outlined her opinions, and then allowed him to sit calmly to outline his. They'd never screamed at one another, not even during the horrendous time when they'd worked hard to get pregnant and failed.

Still, if she got in her truck and returned to Indiana, what then? Eloise knew Greta. She knew, now that she and Eloise were reunited, Greta would come after her if she fled. Beyond that, there was nothing left for her there. She felt like an island.

Eloise remembered the last time she'd ever seen Herb in the flesh. It had been four months before she'd been sent away, and both of them had known they were nearing the end of the line. By that time, Eloise's parents had kept her on a very short leash, which had required Herb to climb up the tree outside her window and come through undetected. It had been a feat worthy of a sitcom. If only the entire event hadn't made Eloise so sad.

That night, sixteen-year-old Herb had suggested many things. He'd said they should take off for elsewhere, that they should hide out until her parents calmed down. But Eloise had been so terrified, unsure of her own feelings and willing, stupidly, to trust in her parents' feelings, instead. She'd kissed Herb for the last time with tears in her eyes and told him that everything that was about to happen was for the best. Back then, mental health wasn't a topic people spoke about, and Eloise wouldn't have been able to define "depression" in the slightest. Looking back, she now knew that's what it was that plagued her. She was so alone and so violently sad.

Around three that morning, Eloise received a sudden text message. It was from Anna.

ANNA: Hey. I can't sleep. Can you?

Eloise smiled sadly to herself.

ELOISE: How did you know?

ANNA: I wish we could calm ourselves down enough for a normal night's sleep.

ELOISE: Me too.

ELOISE: How are you doing, darling?

ELOISE: I still feel so guilty about how we met.

ANNA: Don't. I'm so glad you're in my life.

ANNA: I went to that party yesterday. It was okay. But I still feel so guilty about having any kind of fun now that Dean is gone. We were supposed to have a lifetime together, and now— I don't know what to think.

ELOISE: I can't even imagine, honey.

ELOISE: But I think it's good you pushed yourself to go to the party.

ELOISE: You don't have to go to every party, and you don't have to meet every new person on this island.

ELOISE: But you do have to remember, somehow, that life keeps going. And that you're worthy of an enormous amount of goodness.

Anna didn't write back for a moment. Eloise stewed in fear, wondering if she'd said something wrong.

ELOISE: I'm sorry if I'm overreaching. I can't begin to understand what you're going through.

ANNA: No, no. It's okay.

ANNA: I just dozed off, actually. Lol.

ANNA: Thank you for your help.

ANNA: Try to sleep, Aunt Eloise. Love you.

Eloise stared at the word "love" Anna had typed, feeling as though it anchored her to the earth. Someone loved her. And actually, she had the sense that if she continued to hang around the Copperfield Family, the rest of them would pour their love onto her, as well.

Eloise typed back a simple "good night and love you, too," and then dropped back on the mattress and stared through the dark. Over the next hours, she faded in and out of sleep, each time awakening with panic. She felt as though she'd forgotten something somewhere. Once, she awoke thinking that she was back on the farm and that she'd left the light on in the kitchen and needed to turn it off. How insane she was!

When the clock on the nightstand hit six, Eloise washed her face in the bathroom and walked downstairs to grab a cup of coffee in the dining area. She'd done her best to fall asleep all night long, and she'd ultimately failed. It wasn't the first time, and it wouldn't be the last.

But when Eloise reached the dining room, she stopped short in the doorway to find that someone else had beaten her. There, seated at a two-person table with a mug of coffee in front of him, was Herb. A shiver raced up and down Eloise's spine. For a long time, she wasn't entirely sure if what she saw was real— if this was actually Herb, him sitting in her hotel dining room, seemingly waiting for her.

Herb lifted his gaze to find hers, and for a moment, they held themselves like that, frozen in time. It seemed that every decision Eloise had ever made had led her here to this anonymous dining room at six in the morning to find Herb.

Herb stood slowly. His face was more wrinkled and shadowed than it had been yesterday, as though he hadn't gotten much sleep either. He then pulled his fingers through his gray hair and said, "I'm sorry for surprising you like this."

Eloise shook her head. "It's good to see you again." She said it before she fully realized what she wanted to say. "I feel like I acted like a fool yesterday."

Herb's smile was comforting. "I was the fool in that situation. Not you."

Eloise tilted her head and took several steps toward his

table. "You look exactly the same," she said, surprising herself again.

Herb laughed. "I do not."

"You do." Eloise paused again, feeling silly yet also open-hearted.

"And you look just as beautiful as the day I first saw you," Herb countered.

Eloise laughed abruptly, then placed her hand over her mouth, embarrassed. "I don't."

Herb took a step toward her, closing the distance between them. Eloise thought she might fall down.

"I never wanted you to leave, Eloise," Herb breathed.

"I didn't want to leave, either. I just had no idea what to do."

Herb nodded. "We were kids."

"We were kids," Eloise repeated.

"And the people who were in charge of our destinies are now dead," Herb said.

Eloise furrowed her brow, on the verge of breaking into tears. "We have a lot to talk about."

"That's why I'm here," Herb said with a soft shrug. "Do you feel ready for it?"

Eloise closed her eyes so that her tears didn't fall. It was finally happening: the conversation she'd dreamt of for fifty years. Although she was terrified, she had to face it. It was time.

Chapter Seventeen

It was early Sunday morning, and Anna was seated at a desk in The Copperfield House library with her computer in front of her and her headphones on. In her ears was the voice of Harriet Thornburg, the woman she'd interviewed on the morning of the Nantucket Daffodil Festival Parade, explaining the intricacies of putting on the Nantucket Festival, why Nantucket made her heart sing, and what she would tell someone who'd never been to Nantucket in the first place.

Anna was hard at work on the article, which she planned to submit to both her editor back in Seattle and, if he didn't want it, another travel editor she was friendly with located on the east coast. As she wrote notes to herself and sculpted the article, she felt a fire burning within her, which served as a reminder that she was worthy of something— that she was actually good at something.

By ten that morning, Anna had finished a second draft and felt ready to have someone's eyes on it. Terrified, but excited, she emailed the draft to Everett out on Orcas Island, explaining her hopes for the article and that she needed his help.

Everett wrote back only an hour later.

Anna,

It's so nice to hear from you! I'm actually on Martha's Vineyard right now, visiting Charlotte, so we're in the same time zone. I'm waving at you from across the Sound.

I wanted to reach out to you after what happened. I don't know how to express how sorry I am. The amount of pain you've had to go through at such a young age is absolutely terrible.

I have a lot of respect for the fact that you want to keep writing during this time. Perhaps you agree with me when I say: to write is to live. It's the only way I process my emotions; it's the only way I make sense of the world around me.

Of course, a Nantucket Daffodil Festival isn't the most complex of festivities and therefore doesn't have as much "grit" as some travel writers often look for. But in the article you've written, you paint a portrait of a very charming and historical island, one that upholds its natural beauty, its community, and its traditions. You've created density where many lesser writers wouldn't have known how. I admire that, truly.

One note I have is that I feel Harriet doesn't talk enough about herself here. She talks about her love for the island, about her love of tradition— but not about Harriet Thornburg in the flesh. As you know, what makes a travel article sing is the individual nature of people within these locations. If I were you, I would ask Harriet for a second interview to really broaden the final few paragraphs of the article.

Again, Anna, it's a pleasure to know you and to count myself as a sort of colleague in this insane world we call "travel writing." Please, don't hesitate to send me any additional drafts and reach out for my assistance. I have a hunch that soon, perhaps in only a few years, I'll be reaching out to you for help instead.

All the best,
Everett

Anna closed her laptop and cracked her knuckles, her mind whirring. With Everett's advice, the article seemed to open up for her like a flower, and she understood exactly where to take it to give it that extra "oomph." Before she could overthink it, she grabbed her cell and called Harriet, trying her darnedest not to feel self-conscious about asking for a second interview. She knew that journalists did this kind of thing all the time.

Harriet answered Anna's call on the second ring. "Harriet Thornburg speaking?"

Anna made sure her voice was friendly. "Hi, Harriet. It's Anna Crawford. We met yesterday morning for an interview."

"Of course! Hi, Anna. Gosh, I should apologize to you for Saturday. I was probably acting like a crazy person. Did anything I say make any sense?"

"You were fantastic," Anna assured her. "I couldn't have asked for a better interview, honestly."

"Gosh. I find that hard to believe, but thanks for saying so," Harriet said. "By the way, I think my son said he met you yesterday afternoon. Jack?"

"We did meet, yes." Anna smiled at the memory of the very kind young man who'd actually made her feel like she didn't have two heads.

"I hope he didn't give you any trouble?"

Anna laughed, genuinely adoring Harriet's sense of humor. "Not at all. To be honest with you, I'm the one that's causing trouble."

"How so?" Harriet asked.

"I realized I didn't ask all the questions I needed to ask you," Anna said. "And I was curious if you have any time for a second, short and sweet interview."

Harriet's laughter twinkled. "I would love it. What a pleasure to just get to sit around and talk about the Nantucket Festival I love so much!"

Anna was so grateful that Harriet hadn't made her feel bad. "Thank you so much. Where should we meet?"

"You're at The Copperfield House, correct?" Harriet asked.

"I am."

"I could swing by The Copperfield House in about an hour?" Harriet suggested.

"If it's not too much trouble," Anna said.

"It's not too much trouble at all," Harriet assured her. "Besides. I've always been eager to see inside that house. I used to think it was haunted when I was younger."

Anna laughed gently. "It sort of is haunted, in a way."

"Oh! I'm intrigued about that," Harriet said. "I'll see you in an hour, Anna. Make sure the ghosts save their performance for me."

Chapter Eighteen

Very soon after Herb and Eloise's reunion in the dining room of the hotel, several tourists arrived for breakfast. They were older married couples in for the Daffodil Festival, or they were families with children who couldn't sleep well, or they were young couples who'd come to the island to hike. Regardless of who they were and how kind they were, Eloise and Herb weren't keen to go through the trauma of their past when surrounded by so many strangers. They quickly finished their cups of coffee, then hurried upstairs to Eloise's hotel room.

But once in Eloise's hotel room, the words didn't come. Eloise stared at him, at her previous best friend and dearest love, as he sat at the edge of her unmade bed, and she couldn't help but think about all the years they'd lost, about what kind of person she might have been if only they'd been able to stay together. During these thoughts, she cursed herself, knowing that life turned out just the way it was supposed to— and that Liam had given her a wonderful life. Still, she couldn't help but think about these things. She supposed that was natural.

"These overalls were just about the only thing that survived the fire at my farm," Eloise said when she couldn't think of anything else to say.

"A fire?" Herb's eyes widened. "Gosh, that sounds hard."

"It just happened," Eloise explained. "I think I'm still processing it."

Herb frowned. "Were you there at the time?"

"I had gone into town to go shopping," Eloise explained. "When I turned the corner on our country road, I smelled smoke and just knew, in my gut, that the fire had to be at the farm. When I got a bit further down the road, I saw it up in flames."

Herb shook his head sadly. "I'm so sorry." He then said, "You said, 'our country road.' Who is *we* in that scenario?"

Eloise hadn't realized she'd said "our." Her cheeks burned with embarrassment. "I'm sorry. My husband died three years ago, but I still catch myself saying 'our' and 'we.'"

"It's a difficult habit to break," Herb affirmed.

Eloise sat in the chair in the corner, too frightened of Herb to be closer to him. "Were you a 'we'?"

Herb nodded. "My ex-wife left about twenty years ago."

Eloise had to stifle a shriek. *How on earth could anyone leave Herb— the perfect man!*

"I'm sorry to hear that," she said instead.

Herb lifted his shoulders. "We were only married for about ten years."

"Still, that's enough time to become a 'we,'" Eloise said.

"I suppose so," Herb said.

After that, Herb and Eloise stared at one another for a terribly silent minute, neither sure of what to say. The tension in the room mounted to such a degree that Eloise thought she might choke on the air.

"Do you want to go for a walk?" Herb asked suddenly.

Eloise breathed a sigh of relief. "That sounds nice."

121

Clearly, he sensed how difficult the air was to breathe, as well, but because he was Herb, he knew how to solve the problem at hand. Eloise had missed this about him.

In the parking lot of the hotel, Eloise pointed at the enormous truck. "That's mine," she explained.

Herb laughed with delight. "It's not. Is it?"

"Sure is. My husband died, and I kept the thing. I feel very powerful behind the wheel."

"I've never driven anything half as large," Herb said.

Eloise gave him a sneaky smile. "Do you want to try it now?"

Herb's lips parted with surprise. "Are you sure?"

Eloise jangled her keys from her pocket and tossed them over. Herb reacted quickly and caught them. "What if I wreck it?"

Eloise laughed. "You won't."

"But what if I do? You won't forgive me."

"I just lost almost everything I own in the fire," Eloise reminded him. "If you wreck it, I'll just get something new. Everything is replaceable."

Eloise hadn't sat in the passenger seat of the truck since before Liam's death. There, she stretched the seatbelt over her chest and smiled at Herb as he adjusted the seat to his liking. He puffed out his cheeks, then started the engine. "Here we go," he said.

Herb had always been an excellent driver, even long back before he'd gotten his license. "Remember when we used to steal your father's car and take it for long drives?" Eloise said with a laugh. "We couldn't have been more than fourteen at the time."

"I think Dad always knew," Herb said. "I don't know why he let us get away with it."

"Because you were always so responsible," Eloise

answered. "Everyone trusted you, even when you were that young."

"They didn't trust me later on," Herb reminded her.

To this, Eloise remained silent, unsure of what to say.

For a little while, they remained quiet, darting out of town and out toward the rolling hills of daffodils and the beaches they'd once loved. When the silence got too powerful, Eloise turned on the radio, and, miraculously, The Beatles' "She Loves You" was on, as though the past had come up to bite them and remind them of where they'd come from.

"I can't believe it," Herb said with a laugh.

Eloise smiled and bit her lower lip. After a long pause, she said, "I couldn't listen to The Beatles for years."

"Me neither," Herb told her, his smile falling. "It hurt too much."

Eventually, Herb parked the truck at the edge of a gorgeous beach, then got out and beckoned for Eloise to follow. It was now, miraculously, late in the morning, nearing noon, and April sunlight was powerful and glittering across the sands. Eloise hurried toward him and walked alongside him, her hand swinging just a few inches from his. Again, just in case, she checked his left hand for any sign of a wedding ring, then remembered he'd told her that his wife had left many years ago. *Was his ex-wife insane? Hadn't she known what she'd had?*

"I can't believe you've been in Nantucket all this time," Eloise said softly, surprising herself by getting so close to the subject they both seemed bent on avoiding.

Herb glanced her way, his expression pained. "You should have been here, too."

Eloise remained silent.

"I tried to look for you," Herb continued.

"When?" Eloise was surprised.

"When I was eighteen," Herb explained. "I finally got it out of your father where you'd gone, and I called your Aunt Maude. But she told me that you had gone to community college and that you'd met someone else. She told me to leave you alone."

Eloise's throat was tight. "And you listened to her?"

"No," Herb said. "I did everything I could to find you after that. I called several community colleges in her area. I scoured telephone books. But after a year of searching, my parents begged me to give it up and move on. It seemed clear to everyone that you didn't want to come back to Nantucket."

Eloise's eyes filled with tears. She'd always thought that Herb had washed his hands of her.

As they walked in silence, a dramatic wind surged off the Nantucket Sound and ripped through their gray hair. Eloise was reminded of a long-ago day when they'd walked just like this, swapping stories about Paul, John, George, and Ringo as though they were their dearest friends. How could she create a portal and go back to that day—before so many things had changed?

"Gosh." Eloise stopped short on the beach and peered down along the water. "I didn't realize we were so close to The Copperfield House."

Herb laughed gently. "I hadn't realized we'd been walking for so long."

"When I'm with you, it's like time doesn't exist in the same way. Does that make sense?"

Herb locked eyes with her. "I always felt like that when we were teenagers. It's weird to feel it again. I thought I'd left that way of thinking deep in the past. But here it is. It must just be you. You're the secret to time travel."

Eloise's cheeks burned with embarrassment. "I'm not the secret to anything."

Herb and Eloise remained staring at one another as the Nantucket Sound winds cut through them and wrinkled their jackets. Eloise felt the question billow up from her stomach and surge into her mouth. Before she could stop it, it entered the air.

"Did you ever find out what happened to her?"

Herb's eyebrows were low. "What do you mean?"

Eloise was nervous, shivering. "Our baby. What happened to our baby after we gave her up for adoption? I asked about her at the downtown records office, but Jeremy Farley said there was nothing."

Herb's eyes swam with tears. His face was tight, filled with wrinkles, and he turned to continue walking down the beach, as though he wanted to run away from the question. This filled Eloise with dread.

"Herb, please. Tell me. What happened to her?" Eloise begged, her voice a whisper. "I've dreamed of her every single day. I was never able to have children with Liam, even though we wanted them so badly. She's the only baby I ever had. She's it. And my love for her is so hard to carry because there's so much I don't know about her."

Already, they were nearly in front of The Copperfield House. Herb remained quiet, his feet moving forward through the sands. His face was gray with panic.

"I imagine her as a teacher or a lawyer or a musician or..." Eloise stuttered with disbelief, unsure of how to illustrate any of this pain. "I never even told Liam about her because I didn't want him to know that he was the problem. It was his fault that we couldn't get pregnant. And that was okay! I told myself that God had other plans for us."

Eloise was rambling, and she felt that Herb no longer wanted to hear anything she said. But then, just as Herb turned to her, his eyes strange, there came the sound of a woman from the back porch of The Copperfield House.

"Dad? Dad, is that you?"

Herb raised his chin with surprise, and his face went slack.

Eloise turned, expecting to see one of the Copperfields in conversation with Bernard. But instead, two people popped from the back porch of The Copperfield House— first Anna and then a woman Eloise didn't recognize, perhaps in her late forties. The woman had dark hair and a beautiful smile. And she raised her hand and waved it excitedly at Herb, who could do nothing but raise his hand in return and wave back.

Suddenly, it was as though ten rocks had dropped into Eloise's stomach. She felt as sure of this as she had the day of the fire, when, the moment she'd smelled it, she'd known it was her farm aflame.

"Herb," Eloise breathed. "Don't tell me that's her."

Eloise was suddenly terrified. Slowly, Herb dropped his chin in affirmation, and Eloise closed her eyes against the pain.

Eloise's knees nearly gave out beneath her. For a long and terrible moment, she stared at Herb, who couldn't look at her. Off to the right, the woman who was, impossibly, her daughter and Anna were walking toward them through the sand, and Eloise had the sense that everything in her life was about to explode.

"Dad, what are you doing out here?" The woman was all smiles. When Eloise finally forced herself to look at her, to really look at her, she realized that she looked every bit the way Eloise had about sixteen years ago. There was no mistaking it.

But how could this be?

"I couldn't do it, Eloise," Herb breathed, his eyes very small and filled with certainty. "I couldn't give her up for adoption. I fought your father tooth and nail, and I finally won."

Eloise returned her gaze to the woman before her as her heart thudded with terror. Bit by bit, the woman's smile fell from her face, as though she recognized the weight of this moment. Anna soon caught up to her, and almost immediately, her smile dropped, as well.

"Hi, Aunt Eloise." Anna's eyes turned from Herb to Eloise

to Eloise's daughter, incredulous. "This is Harriet Thornburg. I've been interviewing her for the article I've been writing about the Nantucket Daffodil Festival."

"Harriet Thornburg," Eloise repeated, extending her hand to Harriet's.

Harriet smiled nervously and took Eloise's hand. Perhaps she, too, had sensed the resemblance, even if she didn't fully understand why. "How do you two know each other?" Harriet asked, her voice breaking.

Herb brought his fingers through his hair and seemed at a loss for what to say. In the strange silence, the realization formed in Harriet's eyes, and her lips formed a round O.

"It can't be," she whispered.

Beside Eloise, Herb nodded gingerly. "I had no idea she'd be here, honey. Nor that you'd be here, at The Copperfield House."

Harriet gasped into her hands and gazed at Eloise. Eloise had never been looked at like that before— as though she was the answer to somebody's prayers. It suddenly occurred to her that for every day she'd spent thinking about her daughter, her daughter had been thinking about her, too.

It seemed miraculous.

"Wait." Anna took a step back from the three of them, her face marred with shock. "Wait..."

Eloise raised her hand and placed it on Anna's shoulder. "There's a lot about the past that I find difficult discussing."

Anna's eyes were heavy with tears. She slipped her hand around Eloise's and whispered, "I'm going to make you three tea. Or coffee?" She stuttered with disbelief, then said, "What do you need? What can I get you?"

To this, Harriet laughed gently.

"Anna, we don't need anything but time," Harriet said.

Eloise slid her hand into Harriet's and felt the skin of her palm sizzle. There was such intensity in her daughter's gaze.

"Harriet, my name is Eloise," she heard herself say. "I never imagined I would ever get to meet you. Yet here you are, after so, so long."

"Right back at you," Harriet whispered. "I don't even know what to say."

Chapter Nineteen

After a stunted and strange hour of tea, it was decided that Eloise and Harriet needed space to roam the beach alone as mother and daughter— to finally have time together after decades apart. Herb remained on the back porch of The Copperfield House, his face a mix of fear and joy. He raised his hand at his daughter and his ex-love as they walked back down to the sands, where the wind roared in their ears. Anna busied herself, clearing the teacups and plates of untouched cookies, her face matching Herb's nerves.

"This has been quite an afternoon," Eloise said. She then immediately burst into laughter, feeling that what she'd said was just about the silliest thing anyone could say. "I'm sorry. I don't know what I'm saying or doing."

"Neither do I." Harriet's laughter joined Eloise's, and Eloise thought it was the most beautiful sound she'd ever heard.

For a moment, they walked in silence, their hands shoved in their jacket pockets.

"Anna's a sweet girl," Harriet said simply. "I had no idea I was related to her."

"I suppose she's your second cousin," Eloise said, then shook her head. "My entire life, it seemed like it was just going to be Liam and I. And now, I find myself with all this family around me. And you." She stopped again and stared at her daughter. The sight of her face was enough to break her heart all over again.

Harriet's lower lip shivered with sorrow. "I feel like I have so many questions for you."

"I feel the same," Eloise said.

"What do you want to ask first?" Harriet asked.

Eloise lifted her shoulders. "I don't even know."

Harriet chuckled.

"Why don't you just start telling me about your life?" Eloise suggested. "Start from wherever you like."

Harriet's eyes widened. "Are you sure?"

"Tell me a story that lasts twenty hours, at least," Eloise joked. "I want to hear every single part of your life. Don't leave anything out."

"If you insist," Harriet said. "Well. Let's see. I suppose my memories started when I was three or four, back when we lived with my grandma and grandpa on Dad's side."

"How long did you live with them?" Eloise asked, remembering how kind Herb's parents had always been.

"We moved out when I was six or seven," Harriet explained. "That was around the time I figured out how much younger my father was than most fathers. Which, back then, was really fun for me, you know? Because Dad was always up for a game or to run around. He always had so much energy. Gosh, thinking back to when I was six, he must have only been twenty-two or so. Just a kid, really. My son, Jack, is older than that."

"Anna's older than that," Eloise added.

"Right." Harriet sighed.

"So, it was a happy childhood?" Eloise asked, her voice breaking.

"It was very happy," Harriet affirmed. "Although I knew there was something missing."

Eloise's stomach tightened with fear. "You didn't have a mother."

"Right." Harriet's face was difficult to read. "I know Dad looked for you for a while."

"It was a different time. People weren't so easy to find." Eloise paused for a moment, searching her mind for something to say— something that could possibly make up for so many years of silence.

"Did you ever..." Harriet began to speak, then dropped her gaze to the sand, as though the words were too powerful, too painful to speak.

"I thought about you every single day," Eloise breathed.

Harriet blinked back tears. Because Harriet's face was so similar to Eloise's, Eloise had the sensation that she watched herself cry in the mirror.

"Your father and I were so young when I got pregnant," Eloise said, her voice very quiet. "Which shouldn't have been a problem, you know? Teenage pregnancies happen, and people get through them and go on to raise happy, healthy babies. But my father was not an easy man. Always, he was cruel to me, finding new and creative ways to ensure I knew just how unremarkable I was in his eyes."

"That's terrible," Harriet said.

"I knew the pregnancy would solidify his belief that I was good for nothing," Eloise said. "So, I convinced your father to hide the pregnancy for a little while. I had this idea that we could run away together, have our baby, and start a new life. It was, of course, a ridiculous idea.

"One afternoon, I thought Herb and I were alone at my

parents' house. This wasn't allowed in the first place. I was hardly allowed to have friends over, let alone my boyfriend... especially not when my parents weren't home. We were talking in the kitchen about my plan to run away when, out of nowhere, my mother walked in. Apparently, she'd been napping in the study next door, where she'd woken up and heard everything. By that point, I was four months pregnant and doing everything I could to hide it— wearing baggy shirts and big pairs of pants, which people made fun of me for. But now that my mother knew, there was no hiding it anymore."

Harriet nodded, her face pained.

"I don't have to keep telling this story," Eloise said quietly.

"No. I want to hear it," Harriet said. "Dad has never been able to talk about it."

"After that, my life became a living hell," Eloise said. "My mother called my father home from wherever he was— at the golf club, I think. And he spent the next several hours screaming at me. Afterward, he called Herb's parents and your grandparents and asked them to come over. There, in my living room, my father talked to my boyfriend's parents about my body as though it was a separate entity from me. It was bizarre to feel that although the baby in my womb was mine, something that was growing within me, nobody thought to ask my opinion on anything. All the while, Herb sat there, staring at his shoes, in complete shock. I suppose we both were in shock."

"How did my grandparents act?" Harriet asked softly.

"They weren't pleased," Eloise remembered. "I think everyone's first reaction was just, *'What will people think?'* You know, Nantucket can be like that— overly obsessed about image. I know this firsthand."

"It can still be like that," Harriet affirmed. "No matter how often I try to combat it, I still find myself sucked up in the social vortex sometimes."

Eloise grimaced. "Together with Herb's parents, my

parents decided that the baby, our baby— you, Harriet, would be given up for adoption immediately after the birth. I had absolutely no say in anything. I asked if I could help pick out the parents who would raise my baby, but my father refused."

"But this was still so early in your pregnancy," Harriet whispered.

"Four months," Eloise said. "Which meant I had five more months to be ridiculed by my father and my peers as I grew bigger and bigger. Day after day, I fell into a depression that seemed to grow deeper and deeper. Of course, back then, we didn't have the language for such a diagnosis. Everyone just saw me as the 'problem teenager,' the girl who'd made a 'big mistake.' And that was that."

Harriet stopped on the sand and traced her big toe through it thoughtfully, her eyebrows threading together. "It's so silly what adults blame children for. You were sixteen years old. I didn't know anything when I was sixteen."

Eloise's heart opened up at the forgiveness in her daughter's voice.

"What was Dad doing during that time?" Harriet finally managed to ask, her voice very small.

"I wasn't allowed to see Herb very often," Eloise answered. "My father was making arrangements for me to leave the island to live with my Great Aunt Maude, and he said it was best that I cut all contact. Because Herb and I were at school together, we managed to sneak off sometimes to talk— but we were both so frightened about what had happened and what my father planned to do that our conversations were never the same. The magic had gone."

"That makes sense."

"I took the entire month before your birth off from school," Eloise continued. "I hid in my bedroom, reading and writing in a journal. I couldn't believe that my life had come to this. I knew that I was going to miss Nantucket so much, and I didn't even dare go outside to see it a final time before I had to leave, as I felt it would hurt too badly."

Eloise paused as tears streamed down her cheeks. "I'm sorry. I hope this story isn't too painful to hear. I've never told it to anyone, and I don't know if I'm saying everything correctly."

Harriet locked eyes with Eloise. "You've never told anyone?"

Eloise shook her head.

"Not a therapist? Not your husband?"

Eloise shook her head again. "I was so ashamed of myself. My father infected my head and made me so, so sure that what I'd done was wrong. By the time I went into labor, I felt so outside of my body and so depressed that I felt like I had witnessed the entire birth from above. Of course, the pain was excruciating, but I felt that I deserved that, too."

Harriet's eyes glinted. It was probably traumatic to learn the true horrors she'd come from.

"After you were born, I was left in a room by myself to sleep. Nobody came to see me for many hours. Finally, my mother came, and she told me that my baby had been given up for adoption, that it was over. I cried for so long, but I knew there was nothing I could do. I was just a kid, up against forces I didn't understand."

"When did they send you to your Great Aunt Maude's?"

"Just a week later," Eloise said. "I wasn't even recovered from the birth, and already, I found myself in a new classroom in a new part of the country, battered and bruised and missing Herb desperately. I wasn't allowed to do anything after school except return to Aunt Maude's, where I had numerous chores to finish every single day. Often, I had dreams about my baby— about you, and decided to make up a story that you were with two wonderful parents who loved you and wanted the best for you. In my mind, your parents wouldn't have ever sent you away for making a mistake like mine had."

Harriet's eyes glinted with tears. "And you were right. My father never would have sent me away."

Eloise closed her eyes. "I can't believe you were here all this time. I could have stayed here and helped raise you. I could have been by Herb's side through all of this."

Harriet reached for Eloise's hand. "It sounds like you didn't have a choice. Like you said, your father did everything he could to get you away from here immediately after my birth."

"It sounds like your father had to fight my father to make sure you weren't adopted," Eloise breathed. "I imagine his parents had a big say in that, too." She lifted her eyes to Harriet's, then added, "I imagine they took one look at you and immediately fell in love with you. How couldn't they? And doesn't it speak to the evils of my family that they took one look at you and wanted to send you away as quickly as they could?"

Harriet's chin quivered with sorrow. "I'm so sorry this happened to you."

Eloise shook her head. "I'm so sorry I wasn't there."

For a long time, they held one another's gaze, both overwhelmed with the immensity of this moment. Eloise brushed the tears from her cheek and tried to laugh, remembering, "I stole the conversation out from under you. If I remember correctly, I'd just asked you to tell me everything about your life! Not the other way around."

Harriet shook her head. "I've been wanting to ask you those questions my entire life."

Eloise sighed. "And I suppose I've needed to talk about it my entire life." She paused for a moment, considering if she wanted to share something else. "My husband and I tried for many years to get pregnant, but it never happened for us. I wanted to raise a child so desperately because I felt my baby had been taken away from me."

"Your parents literally robbed you of happiness," Harriet said. "It was a horrible crime."

Harriet sniffed. "But you're here. And you're so beautiful, and you're safe, and— and you said you have a son?"

"I have three children," Harriet explained with a soft smile. "Jack, Margot, and Cassie."

"And your husband?" Eloise asked.

Harriet's eyes darkened. "He passed away a few years ago."

Eloise's jaw dropped. "Oh, Harriet. Oh, no."

Harriet nodded as her shoulders drooped forward. "My husband was a wonderful man. Very kind and considerate and open-hearted. Like you and my father, my husband was my high school sweetheart, and we married when we were a little too young and a little too optimistic."

"I don't know if anyone can ever be too optimistic," Eloise said.

Harriet smiled. "He died in a car accident off the island. He was away on business. Since then, the children and I have been reeling— unsure where to turn or how to handle this new reality." She raised her shoulders, then added, "But I suppose you know all about that, don't you? Because you lost your husband, too."

Eloise considered the fact that, after Liam's death, she'd told her friends back in Muncie that Liam hadn't been "the love of her life." In her mind, always, Herb had been that.

Then again, Liam had been her love, her life, her everything, for decades. He'd left a Liam-sized hole in her heart, which would remain there forever.

"Losing Liam was a terrible thing," Eloise agreed. "I wasn't sure how to stand on my own two feet after that."

"Maybe we can help each other stand up," Harriet offered.

Eloise could hardly believe her ears.

"I mean, if you plan on sticking around," Harriet finished. "I know you haven't lived on Nantucket since you were a teenager. I'm sure the place doesn't really feel like home anymore."

Eloise closed her eyes. "I've dreamed of Nantucket almost every night since I left fifty years ago. When I first drove off the ferry, I had the sensation that none of the past fifty years had happened at all— that it had all been a nightmare that I was now waking up from. And now, I'm standing here in front of my daughter, knowing that I can't possibly go anywhere else. This is my home. This is my everything."

Harriet shook her head delicately, as though she couldn't believe her eyes. "I can't wait to introduce you to everyone."

"And I can't wait to meet everyone," Eloise said. She sniffed again and then quivered with laughter. "But Harriet! I cut you off again. I want to hear more about your childhood. More about everything!"

"Mom, we have time for that!" Harriet returned.

Eloise's ears rang like a gong. "Mom." It was a term she'd never heard associated with herself. She nearly fell to her knees at its power.

In the distance, Herb hurried down from the steps of the porch of The Copperfield House and waved his hands wildly in the air. Eloise pointed, and both Harriet and Eloise waved back.

"I guess we should go see what's the matter," Eloise suggested.

Harriet nodded, and together, they walked through the sharp breeze back toward The Copperfield House. There, Herb's eyes were rimmed with red, but his smile was bright.

"I'm sorry to bother you," he said. "But Greta won't stop pestering me to bring you both in here for dinner. She's been hard at work for hours, and she refuses to let anyone else sit down at the table until you're both seated."

Harriet and Eloise bubbled with surprised laughter.

"Greta?" Eloise stepped through the back porch and headed toward the kitchen. A strong aroma floated from the sizzling pots and pans.

Behind Eloise, Harriet walked along, as though, now that she'd discovered her mother, she wasn't prepared to let her go. Eloise was reminded of mother and baby ducks who waddled together, always connected.

In the kitchen, Greta appeared within a cloud of steam. Her hair was wild and curly around her ears, and her eyes were manic, as though she felt this had to be the very best meal anyone had ever prepared.

"Oh, Eloise." Greta took a step through the steam, then stopped short when she realized who had followed her inside. "And Harriet. Eloise and Harriet." She shook her head, totally at a loss.

Harriet and Eloise stepped into the kitchen, both wordless. Greta dropped her spatula to the side and swallowed them both in a hug as the two of them cried gently against both of her shoulders.

And in this impossible moment, surrounded by her sister and her daughter, Eloise felt a part of the great tapestry of familial life. She felt a part of the love that came, generation after generation, passed down from parents to children. It was impossible to understand why her parents hadn't wanted to love her the right way; it was impossible to understand why they'd wanted to belittle her so.

But Eloise knew, beyond anything, that she had to let the anger from her past go. Only without that anger could she possibly flourish in the here and now. And already, based on only an hour with her daughter, she had a sense that the future could be nothing but bright.

Chapter Twenty

Anna's editor back in Seattle hadn't been able to publish her article about the Nantucket Daffodil Festival, but he had passed the article on to an editor friend on the east coast who'd written Anna immediately to set up a phone call. "Your writing is incendiary," he'd said over the phone, his voice exuberant. Tears had come to Anna's eyes as she'd listened to herself discuss the very few edits he wanted her to make, along with the date he could publish it, both in print and online.

The article was published in the second week of May, over a month after the fateful day when everything in Anna's life had changed forever. It seemed beyond the bounds of reason that Dean hadn't been on the earth since then. It seemed even more insane that Anna had found a way to keep going. She took it easy— one day at a time, resting when she needed to.

Still, as Anna spread the magazine out across the kitchen table in The Copperfield House to see the title and her name in big, bold print, a shiver raced up and down her spine. Despite the depths of her trauma, she'd still managed to make a piece of art— something that people would read and uphold. And this, beyond anything, made her feel more alive than she had in weeks.

Two afternoons after the article was published, Anna met with Andrea for another session. She told her about the article and about how writing the article had ultimately brought Harriet and Eloise together for the first time since Harriet's birth— and Andrea's jaw nearly fell to the floor.

"I always knew that Harriet didn't know her mother," Andrea said. "But this story is truly sensational."

"They're still dealing with the aftermath of what my great-grandfather did all those years ago," Anna explained. "His cruelty completely altered the course of their lives."

Andrea puffed out her cheeks. "I imagine Eloise didn't have anywhere to turn as a young woman."

"No support network at all," Anna agreed. "She was made to be a total outcast." She paused for a moment, then said, "All my family has done since I returned to Nantucket is make sure I feel loved and safe and comforted. It's made me all the more grateful for what I have."

"And how have you felt about your life in Seattle lately?" Andrea asked.

Anna considered this, remembering the studio apartment with its broken stove and its view of the trashcans out the window. "I almost feel ready to give it up. It was my dream to live in Seattle, and it was my dream to marry Dean and have babies with him. But now that I'm here, carving out a new life for myself, I know that I need to find ways to let the past go in order to make space for the new."

"I hope you know you can be patient with yourself," Andrea added.

"Oh, trust me. I'm in no mood to push myself too far," Anna said. "Slow and steady. One day at a time."

* * *

After her grief therapy appointment, Anna walked into the May sunshine and removed her jacket to stride through the downtown streets with her face lifted. The breeze was sensational, smelling of salt and ice cream and baked bread and fried fish. For a moment, she paused at the corner and allowed herself to bask in the incredible texture of the world around her. How grateful she was to be here and for the life she'd been given— even if it had been shadowed with sorrow.

And in that moment of naivety, as she sat in gratefulness, a thought struck her out of nowhere.

When was her last period?

Anna's eyes popped open with surprise. Slowly, her hand extended over her stomach as she dared to think something that seemed impossible. As moments passed, she did her darnedest to count back the days in her cycle, realizing that she'd bypassed her period by more than two weeks at this point. At the time, she'd been so stricken with grief that she hadn't even noticed.

It was possible that she'd missed it because of stress. Bodies reacted to grief in all sorts of ways.

But another reason was possible, as well.

Oh, the thought terrified and thrilled her at once. Abruptly, she turned on her heel and walked back to the drugstore on the corner, where she charged back to the pregnancy tests and stalled in front of them. They all looked approximately the same, with similar prices and similar photographs that advertised happy mothers with vibrant smiles. Unsure, Anna grabbed four different ones and hurried to the counter, where she paid with her card and tried not to look the cashier in the eye. It was strange, she thought now, to reveal so much of your personal life to the cash register at the drugstore.

"Good luck," the woman at the register said as Anna fled the store.

Anna couldn't stop herself before she said, "Thank you!"

She supposed the woman had sensed Anna's excitement. Anna hadn't passed the pregnancy tests over the counter with dread. She'd basically thrown them there with endless enthusiasm, as though they'd been party favors.

All the way back to The Copperfield House, Anna floated, her heart in her throat. She hardly dared to dream the impossible and tried her best to quiet her stirring mind.

When she reached The Copperfield House, she found it in a state of chaos. This wasn't a huge surprise— it seemed that always, people were coming and going from the old Victorian as though it was an open house.

In the front living room, Harriet and her son, Jack, whom Anna had met at the party a couple of weeks back, were in conversation with Ella and Danny. On the opposite side of the room were Alana and Julia, sipping mugs of tea as they chatted about something else. Anna rushed past them, taking special care not to make eye contact with her mother. Julia would know something was up immediately. It was mother's intuition.

"Hi, honey!" Julia called anyway. "Where are you off to so quickly?"

"I'll be right back," Anna returned just before she disappeared up the staircase, hurrying toward the bathroom nearest her bedroom.

Once there, Anna latched the door behind her and gasped at her reflection in the mirror. She looked half-panicked, and the May breeze had tangled her black hair into wild proportion.

"Come on, Anna. Just take the test," she muttered to herself, unwilling to wait around a moment longer, stirring in nerves.

Anna followed the instructions on the test and then waited with her back to the test for a full three minutes. Throughout, she shifted her weight from foot to foot, her anxiety mounting.

When the alarm blared on her phone, Anna turned to blink down at the little test, where, incredibly, two very pink lines had appeared. At first, Anna freaked out, thinking that two lines meant "not pregnant," but when she checked the box, she realized she had it backward. Two lines meant pregnant. It meant that she was carrying Dean's baby in her womb— so many weeks after Dean had left the earth forever.

It was nearly too much to bear.

Anna fell to her knees and pressed her hands over her eyes. Tears welled behind her hands, and she felt herself shaking with a mix of sorrow and gratefulness. This seemed like a gift from the heavens.

When Anna did finally collect herself enough to gather the pregnancy test and leave the bathroom, she was still red-faced with shock. She hadn't heard anyone in the hallway and hadn't assumed anyone was near, but when she opened the door to find Eloise staring at her from the other end of the hallway, her eyes were wide with surprise.

Of course, wherever you went in The Copperfield House, there was someone there, ready to comfort you.

"Anna? Are you all right?" Eloise took a delicate step forward, her eyes glistening.

Anna let out a single sob. *What was the use of keeping this secret to herself? Hadn't there been enough secrets in the Copperfield Family so far?*

Slowly, Anna lifted the pregnancy test in the air and shrugged. "Apparently, I'm pregnant." Her voice was hardly a whisper.

Eloise picked up speed after that, clearing the space along the hallway until she stood before her, peering at the pregnancy test. "My gosh." She shook her head. "It's a miracle. Anna. It really is a miracle." She repeated it, as though the weight of this moment needed another confirmation.

Suddenly, Eloise's arms were around her, and Anna felt her body shake with sobs. Eloise consoled her, wrapping her arms tighter as she whispered, "This is such a gift, Anna. It truly is. And we'll be here throughout the entire process. We won't let you go through this alone."

Anna sniffed and closed her eyes, allowing herself to imagine the baby growing in her womb— perhaps a little boy who looked so much like Dean. In every way, she knew that this baby would serve as a forever reminder of the love she had for Dean. She'd always known that their love was powerful, that it was meant to withstand the test of time. With Dean's death, she'd questioned that. She hadn't known where to put all her love for him, now that he was gone.

As usual, life had its way of stringing her around and altering her best-laid plans.

With this baby, she knew how her love for Dean would continue. And although it was sorrowful, a tragedy that Dean couldn't be there for the birth of his child, it was, in every way, a miracle. She had to remember that.

Chapter Twenty-One

The little cabin on Nantucket was approximately half as big as the farmhouse Eloise had shared with Liam. This, she told Greta as they walked through the door, made it the perfect size for "just her." She removed the keys from the front door and jangled them as she slipped them into her overalls pocket, walking through the kitchen with its gleaming countertops and its view of the rolling hills and forest just outside.

"It's perfect, Eloise." Greta splayed her hand over her chest as her eyes scanned the hills and the daffodils that swayed gently in the breeze.

"I never imagined I'd have my own place in Nantucket," Eloise breathed. "It was almost like I didn't think Dad would allow me to have it." After another beat, she laughed gently and said, "I can't believe how long I let him dictate how I lived. Even so many years after his death."

"He did cast a long shadow," Greta said, eyeing Eloise.

Over and over again, Greta had apologized for not

pestering their parents for more information about what "hor-rible thing" Eloise had done back in the seventies, the act that had gotten her kicked out of the house. And over and over again, Eloise had told Greta it was in the past. She couldn't blame Greta for what had happened— she hadn't been in the country at the time.

And besides, she was so grateful for their newly built friendship that she found herself living in the beauty of the present rather than falling into the shadows of the past. The therapist she'd recently begun to see on Nantucket had told her that was the healthiest way to live. She'd also said that she'd met with many women in their fifties, sixties, and seventies, all of whom had gone through traumatic experiences many years ago — experiences that had been brushed under the rug during a time when mental health wasn't talked about. "It's so good that women are finding the strength to come forward and talk about what has happened to them," the therapist had said.

"This is the first place I've ever chosen for myself," Eloise said, brimming with excitement. "I was always either at Aunt Maude's, or in that sad apartment Aunt Maude picked out for me after I left her house, or with Liam in the farmhouse. But here? This cabin already feels like home."

Very soon afterward, Greta had to head back to The Copperfield House to prepare for Danny and James' baseball game, which she planned to attend with several other members of the Copperfield crew. "Would you like to come along?" Greta asked Eloise as she slipped on her spring jacket.

"I would. But I have plans with Harriet, Jack, Margot, Cassie, and Herb."

Greta's eyes widened with surprise. "Your own family."

"I suppose so." Eloise could hardly believe it herself.

"What's the plan?" Greta asked.

"They're coming here," Eloise explained. "I have a card

table and chairs in the truck. We'll sit out on the porch and eat pizza together."

"It sounds perfect," Greta said.

* * *

Two hours later, Harriet's minivan appeared in the driveway. She waved from the front seat as the first of Eloise's grandchildren popped out from the back. Margot carried a stack of pizzas, as her sister, Cassie, carried two liters of soda, one in each arm. Jack had a bottle of wine in one hand and adjusted a baseball hat on his head as Harriet brought up the rear.

Although she'd seen photographs, Eloise hadn't yet met her grandchildren. As they approached her, Eloise's throat tightened with fear, and she fumbled around her mind for something to say. For some reason, she didn't want to be perceived as a "lame grandmother" during her very first try at being one. Then again, she was sixty-five, and they were young and cool and interesting. There was no way they wouldn't perceive her as "lame."

"Hello!" Eloise smiled warmly as they approached, crossing and uncrossing her arms.

"Hi, Mom." Harriet hurried around her children to hug Eloise tightly. There on the front porch steps, she turned back to place her hand on each of her children's heads as she introduced them. "This is Jack, my eldest. And this is Margot, and this is Cassie. Everyone, this is your grandmother."

The three Thornburg children peered at Eloise curiously. One after another, they mounted the porch steps to hug her, and Eloise's tears thickened with each hug.

"Goodness, it's good to meet you," Eloise breathed, stepping back to allow them past her to sit at the card table.

Before anyone else could speak, Herb's car appeared in the

driveway and parked alongside Harriet's. He then popped out and waved, carrying a six-pack of beer in one hand as he ambled easily toward them. Eloise's heart flipped over at the sight of him.

"Grandpa! Hi!" Eloise's grandchildren hurried to their feet to hug him, and Eloise was warmed by the love they had for this wonderful man.

Herb hugged Harriet next, then turned to smile brightly at Eloise. "There she is," Herb said, as though he saw her every day. "I brought a six-pack."

"Sign me up," Eloise said with a smile as she followed Herb into the kitchen, where he placed four in the fridge and popped the top of two. He passed one beer to her, and they clinked them together, holding one another's gaze.

"I'm terrified of them," Eloise said under her breath.

Herb laughed openly. "You shouldn't be. They're your grandchildren."

"I know that," Eloise said. "But I have no idea how to talk to them. I'm terrified they'll think I'm boring or not worthy or..."

Herb placed his hand on Eloise's shoulder. "You shouldn't think like that. If there's one thing I know about my grandchildren— I mean, our grandchildren— it's that they're kind, good-natured, and lovely people. They're so curious about you, about your life since you left Nantucket. Just be honest with them, and they'll be honest with you."

"Dad? Mom? The pizza's getting cold!" Harriet opened the porch door and waved them both back.

Eloise sat between Herb and Harriet and watched as Jack piled her paper plate with pepperoni and vegetarian pizza slices.

"We'll have to go shopping for essentials," Harriet said to Eloise.

"Goodness, yes. I just signed the paperwork yesterday. I still need so many things!"

"Do you have a bed?" Harriet asked.

"I have a bed," Eloise affirmed. "But that's about it. I still need plates. A kitchen table. Forks!"

Her grandchildren laughed gently.

"Mom loves shopping for all that stuff," Margot explained, casting Harriet a smile.

"Mom loves shopping, period," Jack affirmed.

"That's funny," Eloise said. "I was never so keen on it."

"We'll make it fun," Harriet assured her. "This is your first place on your own in Nantucket! You need to make it your own."

Over the next two hours, Eloise found herself caught in a wonderful ecosystem of family conversation. Margot and Cassie were both incredibly dear, chatting easily about Margot's senior year of high school and Cassie's final few weeks of her sophomore year. Jack and Herb were in business together, apparently, taking tourists out for fishing cruises, which was a job they both spoke of poetically.

"It's so nice to be out on the water with my grandson," Herb said.

"He's taught me everything I know," Jack affirmed.

"You'll have to take me out sometime," Eloise suggested, surprising herself with how forward she was.

"We'd love it!" Herb said.

"Just say the word, and we'll clear the schedule for the day," Jack said.

"Maybe we should all go," Harriet chimed in. "I haven't been out on the water in a while. That Daffodil Festival nearly killed me this year."

"Thank goodness it's over," Margot agreed.

"I get to take a few months off before I have to start planning for next year," Harriet explained. "I plan to make the most of my time off."

As the evening light dimmed to grays and blues and the air

shimmered with spring chill, Eloise and Harriet gathered the empty pizza boxes and the empty cups and deposited them in the kitchen.

"Am I doing okay?" Eloise asked her daughter, surprised at her own naivety.

"You're wonderful!" Harriet squeezed Eloise's arm. "My kids love you."

"Probably not yet," Eloise said. "But hopefully, they'll find a way to love me. Or at least put up with me." She laughed.

But Harriet shook her head. "I know you went through hell when you were younger." She paused, swallowed, then added, "I just hope you can find a way to be kinder to yourself in your head. You deserve kindness, Mom, both from the world and yourself."

Eloise was struck by how profound this sounded. *Why had it never occurred to her that the voice in her head could be so monstrous?*

Soon, Harriet and her children prepared to leave, all promising that they'd return to Eloise's little cottage soon.

"I imagine we'll find excuses to pop by frequently," Harriet said as she hugged Eloise.

"I make cookies," Eloise told her grandchildren, remembering how jealous she'd been of Brenda back in Indiana, who'd baked for her grandchildren.

"We love cookies," Margot assured her as she hugged her.

For a long moment, Herb and Eloise stood on the porch and watched as Harriet drove her children away from the house. All of the grandchildren waved through the windows, and Harriet honked her horn just before they disappeared behind a wall of trees.

And when they were finally gone, Eloise collapsed in a chair and burrowed her face in her hands.

"Hey! Hey." Herb sat beside her and placed his hand on

her upper back. "Eloise, it's okay. It went so well! Didn't you think so?"

But how could Eloise explain what she felt? She felt so excited, so terribly pleased, that she wasn't sure how to say anything without bursting into tears. When she finally removed her hands from her face, all she could do was grin up at Herb like a very happy fool.

"I'm sorry," she said very quietly. "That entire dinner was just beyond my wildest dreams."

Herb laughed. "Mine, too."

Herb stood to grab them two more beers, which they popped out on the porch of the cabin where Eloise would spend the next years of her life. For a little while, they drank in silence, enjoying the beauty of one another's company.

Beneath the surface of the silence, Eloise felt the air thicken with apprehension. Although she didn't dare to hope for it, not really, she sensed something when Herb looked at her. It was as though they were fifteen again, preparing for their very first kiss.

With that first kiss, their entire lives had been uprooted, their world had shifted on its axis, and Eloise had been taken away from her family and left to stir in decades of self-hatred.

But, Eloise thought now, the love between Herb and Eloise had never been the problem. That had been the most nourishing thing she'd known.

Eloise lifted her eyes to Herb's and found that he'd been studying her, too.

"What are you looking at?" Eloise asked with a laugh.

Herb shook his head delicately and took a sip of beer. "I always thought you were the prettiest girl on the island. The more things change, the more things stay the same."

Eloise's cheeks burned with embarrassment. All she wanted was to protest— to tell him that he had it all wrong. She wasn't beautiful, and she was nobody.

151

But in the silence that unfolded after his compliment, Eloise allowed herself to believe, if only for a moment, that she really was as beautiful as he said. And maybe, just maybe, she would allow herself whatever happiness this life allowed her. She just had to be brave enough to accept it.

Chapter Twenty-Two

Julia made Anna an appointment to confirm the pregnancy, where they learned, together, with their hands linked, that Anna was six weeks along. Anna sobbed gently into her hand as she looked at the collection of cells on the screen before her. Dean should have been with her— he should have been the one holding her hand. But instead, it was her mother, Julia, who gazed down at both her and the image of her grandchild with similar tears and eventually said, "That's your baby, Anna. Aren't you already in love?"

After the appointment, Julia and Anna roamed through the sunlight outside the clinic, walking nowhere in particular until they found themselves in front of a seaside restaurant.

"Are you hungry?" Julia asked Anna, her voice soft and sensitive. Anna's hunger was always coming and going, never a sure thing due to her sorrows and trauma.

"I need to feed this baby," Anna said, both hands over her stomach. For the first time since Dean's death, she felt very sure that she needed to sustain herself. Someone else's needs now came far above her own, but they necessitated that she take good care of herself.

Anna and Julia sat on the patio and ordered iced tea and a salad to share, one with goat cheese and spinach and tart dried cranberries. For their main course, Anna ordered a filet of cod, while Julia opted for chicken.

"My baby girl, all grown up and pregnant." Julia smiled and gripped Anna's hand gently on the table.

"You told me a month ago not to have a surprise pregnancy," Anna reminded her. "Because my apartment was too small to accommodate a baby."

"Did I?" Julia shook her head, searching her mind for the memory. "I don't know why I would have ever told you not to have a surprise pregnancy. Surprise pregnancies are the best! It's how your father and I had you, you know."

Anna had heard this many times. She laughed, sipped her iced tea, then furrowed her brow. "But you must have been terrified."

"Absolutely terrified," Julia affirmed. "Your father and I were just two selfish, crazy young people. Maybe we were in love, and maybe we weren't. But when I took the pregnancy test, we looked at each other and realized we had to change some things."

"You weren't much older than Eloise was when she had Harriet," Anna said.

"Very true," Julia said. "There are so many differences between our stories. For one, Eloise is quite a bit older than me. Imagine being pregnant at sixteen in the early seventies."

Anna shivered at the thought. "And her father was so cruel."

"Just awful," Julia agreed.

"What if you had gotten pregnant at sixteen? Do you think Grandma and Grandpa would have handled it well?" Anna asked.

Julia thought for a moment, her eyes on the glowing horizon along the water.

"I know things were already crazy at The Copperfield House," Anna added hurriedly, remembering the horrible trial that had put Bernard in prison.

"It's okay. It's a good question to ask," Julia said kindly. "I'd like to think that my mother would have had compassion for me. But to be honest with you, things were quite intense at my house back then. Artists were always coming and going, becoming something big in the art world, and there was constant pressure to become something, as well. Had I gotten pregnant at sixteen, I think my mother and father would have been very, very disappointed in me. And I hate to say that, but I have a hunch it's true."

Anna frowned. "I have a feeling you wouldn't have been pleased with me, either. And, oh gosh. Imagine what Dad would have said. He wouldn't have talked to me for months."

Julia locked eyes with Anna. "It's so hard to know what would have happened. I'd like to think I would have handled it with grace and love, but who knows? Back when you were a teenager in Bartlett, Illinois, your father and I were so hopeful for your future. I mean, we still are. You're doing wonderfully, honey. And now that you're older, I know you can handle both a career and a baby. If anyone can, you can."

Anna dropped her gaze, thinking again of her father, who'd continued to text her nearly every day since Dean's death. She sipped her iced tea and held the silence for a while as so many stories stirred within her head.

"Something I can't get over," Anna began, "is that Eloise keeps saying she doesn't hold a grudge against her father. That she forgives him for what happened."

Julia raised her eyebrows. "I've thought the same. I don't know if I could forgive someone for that."

"I told myself I never wanted to talk to Dad again," Anna said very quietly.

Julia remained silent.

"Do you think I'll regret it?" Anna breathed. "I mean, what he did to me, to our family, is basically nothing compared to what Eloise's father did to her."

Julia's eyes flickered.

"I just couldn't believe he abandoned you like that," Anna continued, speaking a little too quickly. "It was like he forgot everything we stood for as a family. I'd thought we were strong. That we cared about each other."

Julia nodded very slowly. After a very long pause, she finally spoke. "Your father was never the love of my life, Anna. And maybe it was insincere of me to marry him in the first place."

Anna's lips parted with surprise. Her mother had never said this. "Why did you?"

"I was so young. Gosh, it's like I was a different person." Julia pulled her dark hair into a ponytail. "But by the time we were married, we'd already had you, and we were pregnant with Henry, and it seemed like our lives were running out in front of us without our permission. I figured we should just run forward instead of looking behind. And that worked for a very long time." Julia paused for a moment, then added, "And I don't regret anything that's happened. Because it all led me here— to this restaurant where I'm sitting with you, my pregnant daughter. And just a few streets away, my high school sweetheart is working in his workshop, and our love is stronger than ever."

Anna nodded. "I'm so glad you've found this life for yourself, Mom."

Julia wrapped her hand around Anna's. "Nothing that's happened to you is fair, honey. But in everything, I hope you go with your gut feeling. It can't lead you astray."

Chapter Twenty-Three

Anna hadn't been to New York City in many years. Later that week, when she arrived on the bus and stumbled out into the chaos of Manhattan, she paused for a moment, gasping for breath, astonished at the weight of the dank air and the sounds of the car horns and the penetrating blue sky just above the very tall buildings. Seattle had nothing on New York City, and now that she was an islander, every city seemed to pulse with far too much life and far too much noise. She realized, with a funny jump in her stomach, that city life was behind her now. She was on the path to something else.

Anna checked into a cheap hotel room north of Central Park, where she took a shower to get the bus stink off of her, then dressed in a navy-blue dress and a pair of flats. In the mirror, she gave herself a pep talk as, on her phone, an email from her editor dinged through. They wanted her to go on another trip soon to write about Bar Harbor, Maine. *Was she up for it?* Anna wrote back quickly to say she was and that, given her proximity to anything on the east coast, she was up for a vibrant schedule of travel writing events that summer.

At six-thirty, Anna took the subway to Greenwich Village. There, she walked along gorgeous streets, past townhouses that told her stories of New York eras past, and fell into the daydream of this city's vibrant life.

And then, before she knew what had hit her, she found herself in front of the restaurant where she'd agreed to meet Jackson Crawford. She adjusted her dress in the reflection of the door, then walked through, her heart in her throat.

Already, her father was at the back corner table, wearing a suit and tie, his hair styled with gel. He looked younger and hipper than he had when they'd lived in the suburbs of Chicago, and Anna reminded herself that, although her father would always be her father, he was allowed to build whatever life he pleased. He was a rather young man, still. There was a lot of time left for him to become whatever it was he needed to become.

"Hi, Dad." Anna felt nervous enough to faint. She smiled at him from the other side of the table, then winced as her father sprung to his feet and gathered her in an awkward hug. Anna allowed it to happen, unsure how not to. And after a few moments in his embrace, Anna was cast into memories long past, when she'd just been a girl who'd loved her daddy.

"Anna. Anna, Anna." Her father seemed overwhelmed. Very soon after, he stepped back and sat in the chair, then began to babble about the restaurant, about how he'd always wanted to take her there because they had great dumplings, and how grateful he was that she'd decided to come into the city to see him.

"Thanks for taking time off work," Anna said, feeling herself smile.

"It's not a big deal," Jackson said. "I'm happy to take off work whenever you want to come into the city." He paused, then added, "Maybe sometime you, Henry, and Rachel can all come at the same time. You can even stay at my apartment if you want."

Jackson stalled, realizing he'd pushed it too far. "Anyway. What are you drinking?"

Anna ordered a Diet Coke from the server, and her father ordered a glass of white wine. He then told her how exquisite the wine selection was and that she should really try it, but Anna just shrugged and said, "I don't feel like drinking tonight." This shut her father up immediately.

After they ordered several tapas, including dumplings and crab rangoon and spring rolls, Dean sipped his wine and caught her eye.

"I don't know how to tell you how sorry I am about what happened to Dean."

Anna dropped his gaze, as it was too intense, like looking at the sun. "Thank you for saying that."

"Really, honey. I know you two had plans. And what happened is uniquely unfair."

"Bad things happen all the time," Anna said, wanting to shove away her father's kindness. But instead, she rebounded and said, "Thank you for saying that, though. It means a lot."

"I wish I could have met him," Jackson said. After a long pause, he added, "Would you mind telling me about him?"

This was something nobody had asked Anna, not since Dean's death. She swallowed the lump in her throat and brought the memory of Dean's face back to her mind. Oh, gosh. She loved that face. She loved him so much.

"He was so funny," Anna heard herself say. "We used to laugh and laugh until we couldn't laugh anymore. And he was adventurous, too. He always wanted to try a new restaurant or see a new band in concert or travel somewhere spontaneously. When he asked me to marry him, I thought— wow. My life is going to be so exciting because he'll always be around."

Jackson continued to study Anna with dark eyes, hanging on her every word.

"When he died, I was pretty sure that I was just going to die, too," Anna confessed, her voice breaking. "But now..."

Should she tell him? It was such a huge intimate secret, and yet, a strange part of her needed her father to know.

"What now?" Jackson asked, sounding like he was on the brink of tears, himself.

"I just learned that I'm pregnant," Anna whispered. "It's too early to tell people. But I'm telling you because, well." Her voice continued to waver. "Because I love you. And I missed you. And I know, now, how short life can be."

Jackson's face broke open. He immediately covered it with both hands as his shoulders shook. "Oh, Anna."

Anna wasn't sure where to look. She cupped her hands together until she felt her father reach for her, and then, she took his hand with hers. Together, they sat like that, linked for the first time in a year.

"Thank you for telling me," Jackson said then, his eyes wide open and honest. "I know I don't deserve it."

Anna remained very still.

"I can't apologize enough for how I handled everything last year," Jackson continued. "I got so greedy with my life. I wanted everything to change all at once, and stupidly, for the first time since you kids were born, I was ready to focus only on myself. It should have come as no surprise that you, Henry, and Rachel wanted nothing to do with me after that.

"But I'm so sorry, Anna," Jackson continued. "I've learned so much during this crazy year. Sometimes, I miss your mother more than I can bear to admit, even to myself. She was such a wonderful partner to me for years."

Anna frowned.

"And I know that she's even happier now than she was with me," Jackson continued. "Which is a slap, of course, but one I deserve. Men leave their wives all the time, of course. Arrogant, terrible men like me. But they don't often watch their wives return to 'the one who got away' like that. It's a remarkable and terrible experience."

Anna blushed, recognizing the pain in her father's eyes.

"I just hope that you'll allow me a bit of space in your baby's life," Jackson said. "Again, I know I don't deserve it. But I'd love to know him or her."

Anna's eyes filled with tears. "I'm here, aren't I?"

Jackson lifted his chin.

"I mean, I want to be here. I want to work things out with you." Anna stuttered, on the brink of falling apart. "I know it will take time and effort on both of our parts. But I feel ready to do that. If you are."

Jackson nodded and closed his eyes. And at this moment, Anna remembered a time very, very long past when her father had sat by her bed as she'd fallen asleep – terrified of the night-mares that had plagued her. *I'll be right here, Anna. Don't worry about a thing. Your daddy will keep the nightmares away.*

* * *

It came as no surprise that Grandma Greta had prepared a gorgeous feast for Anna's return. What had begun with "let's just tell a few people about the pregnancy" had soon extended to, "Why not tell all the Copperfields about the pregnancy?" and now, it seemed that the entire house was filled with expectation, swallowing Anna with hugs. Greta hurried Anna to the table, where she poured her a glass of lemon water and told her that the city air was probably very bad for her— that it was better for her to remain on the island from now on.

"How was your dad?" Scarlet sat next to her, wearing a knowing smile.

Anna laughed nervously. "It was weird and really nice to see him."

"It's weird to forgive people, isn't it?" Scarlet said, glancing across the room at her father, who was in the midst of explaining a story, his hands moving wildly around him to illustrate his points.

"It makes me feel so much lighter," Anna confessed. "Only for the time being, of course." She spread her hand across her stomach and winked.

Scarlet laughed outright. "None of us can wait for this baby. I heard Grandma talking about decorating a nursery in The Copperfield House just this morning."

Anna shook her head, incredulous. "It takes a village to raise a child, I guess."

"Have you told Dean's parents about the baby yet?"

"I called them last night after I got back to my hotel in the city," Anna explained. "Dean's mom almost fainted. They're arranging a trip to come out to see me soon."

Scarlet smiled. "It really is a miracle."

A moment later, Eloise, Harriet, Herb, and Harriet's three children arrived, ambling through the door to the dining room with suntanned faces and happy smiles. If Anna wasn't mistaken, she was pretty sure that Eloise and Herb had been holding hands upon their entrance to the dining room, which they immediately dropped. Anna locked eyes with Eloise, remembering the incredible journey they'd both been on since they'd stumbled into one another in that nondescript diner.

"How was the city, honey?" Eloise asked as she slid into the chair on the other side of Scarlet.

Anna placed her hand lovingly on Eloise's shoulder. For the first time in ages, Eloise wasn't wearing her overalls and had instead donned a dark green dress. She looked gorgeous.

"The city was a surprise," Anna answered honestly. "And I think I owe you a thank you."

Eloise cocked her head. "Why?"

"You reminded me that life is full of surprises," Anna continued. "As long as I open my heart to them."

Bernard appeared in the doorway, his arms laden with a platter of glistening turkey, as Greta peered from behind his shoulder, barking instructions. "Everyone! Sit down! Dinner is ready!" And in the wild haze of the next few moments, Anna allowed herself to fall into the chaos, another puzzle piece of the gloriously complicated Copperfield Family. She wouldn't have had it any other way.

Coming Next

Coming Next in the Nantucket Sunset Series

Pre Order A Nantucket Season

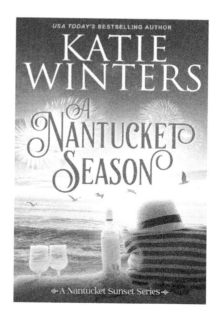

Other Books by Katie

The Vineyard Sunset Series

A Nantucket Sunset Series

Secrets of Mackinac Island Series

Sisters of Edgartown Series

A Katama Bay Series

A Mount Desert Island Series

The Coleman Series

Connect with Katie Winters

BookBub
Facebook
Newsletter

Made in the USA
Monee, IL
16 April 2023

31952552R00095